Mad Dog

Kelly Watt

Also by Kelly Watt

Camino Meditations

Mad Dog

Kelly Watt

Hamilton Stone Editions
Maplewood, New Jersey, U.S.A.

Library of Congress Cataloging-in-Publication Data

Watt, Kelly.
  Mad dog / by Kelly Watt.
      pages ; cm
  ISBN 978-0-9903767-0-5 (alk. paper)
  I. Title.
  PR9199.4.W38M33 2015
  813'.6--dc23

                                        2015011758

Hamilton Stone Editions
P. O. Box 43
Maplewood, New Jersey 07040
www.hamiltonstone.org

Book Design by WSM Technical
Cover image: @iStock.com/Byrdyak

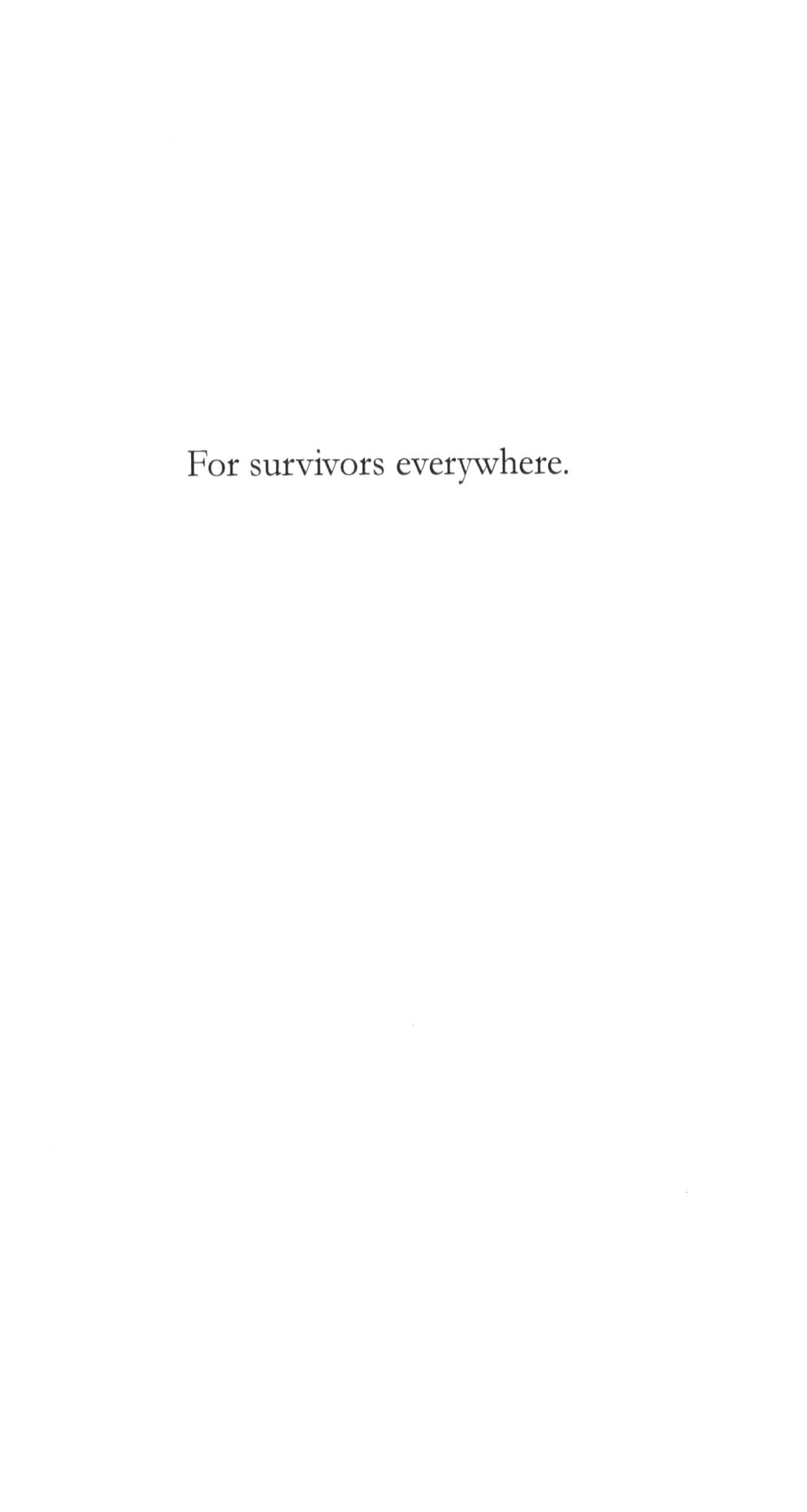

For survivors everywhere.

Mad Dog

Kelly Watt

O goodness infinite, goodness immense!
That all this good of evil shall produce,
And evil turn to good.

      - John Milton, *Paradise Lost*

Introduction

This spring, 2019, I finally decided to reprint a revised edition of my first novel *Mad Dog* in the U.S. with Hamilton Stone Editions, partly to keep the novel in print, but also because the #metoo movement of 2017/18 had given me renewed hope. When I first wrote about childhood sexual abuse in the 1990s, a pall surrounded the topic and the authors who dared to write about it. My first novel came out during the height of the false memory syndrome movement, essentially a backlash movement aimed at feminists and activists, who were trying to bring forth stories of violence against women and children. The backlash was largely successful, to the despair of many. As a result, I often felt in those days, that the shame of the issue fell on the messengers rather than the perpetrators.

The small town that I describe in this novel could have been any number of small towns in Ontario. Cedar Hollow is a town of hierarchies, and children are not the only people exploited there. The Indigenous characters in the book are often referred to as "Indians," and Harry Madeleine as a "Negro," which was common parlance at the time. Although these words are no longer politically correct, the book takes place in 1964 and the narrator is only fourteen, and mimics the adults around her. So after long deliberation, I decided to keep the usage. To change it would be disingenuous or dishonest somehow—a literal act of whitewashing. I beg your pardon for any offense, and ask you to read with the context and my good intentions in mind.

In recent years, sexual assault victims have begun to come forward, and some have been heard. There's been a massive paradigm shift around these issues for the better. But I feel it's important to remember that victims of childhood sexual abuse in generations past, mostly suffered in silence and without recourse to justice, compensation, protection, dignity or even respect. Their lives were a post traumatic struggle, rife with revictimization and secondary trauma. I have decided to reissue this book not just for me, but also for them.

Kelly Watt, February 2019

Prologue

In the dream it is the girl's birthday. She is three. It has only been a few months since her mother got into her blue car and drove away. To celebrate the girl's birthday, the grey mare is saddled up. The girl struts about in white cowboy boots like a cowgirl. Her hair is in pigtails and tied with pink ribbons. She wears a matching pink dress with white butterflies on the front that her mother will never see.

The mare stands quietly by the fence in the sun, her tail rhythmically thwacking flies, skin twitching. A tall man hoists the girl onto the saddle and walks her around the riding ring while the girl chatters to Eponey. It is spring and the fields glow emerald in the sunlight. The sun is hot on the girl's raven hair and the smell of spring flowers mingles with the mare's sweet horsy smell. A window is open and a breeze blows the lace curtains lazily in and out. The record player has been pulled up to the window and the man hums along to a song by Nat King Cole. The trio circles the ring again and again. It is a happy day, the happiest day in a long time it seems.

Afterwards, the man takes their picture. For a moment, the picture is frozen in the girl's mind: the snapshot of the horse and herself as a little girl with the apple on her palm. Everything in black and white.

July

Nauta agricolae cancrum dat; agricola, malum nautae.

(The sailor gives the farmer a crab;
the farmer (gives) the sailor an apple.)

The first time Sheryl-Anne saw Peter Angelo was in the summer of 1964. The Summer of Freedom and race riots, the summer everyone argued about the maple leaf. That summer Sheryl-Anne MacRae was fourteen.

He arrived one hot afternoon in July, while she was lying in her favourite tree, listening to Motor City's Motown Hour. All day long the cicadas had been whining in the heat. Sheryl had dozed off momentarily and dreamed, awakening to Dr. Beat crooning into her ear: *Now here's a witty ditty from our favourite high school girls from across the border* ... and Diana Ross, the queen of all girls that summer had come on singing, "When the Lovelight Starts Shining in his Eyes."

Then her uncle's Pontiac came up the drive. Sheryl hung her transistor on a branch and pressed the binoculars to her eyes. The orchard zoomed into view along with the weathered cedar grey barn and the gardening shed with its metal corrugated roof, where her eleven-year-old cousin Joshua crouched in the dirt playing war, mimicking explosions and gunfire. Sheryl could see the Victorian house with its steep gables and gingerbread trim, its wide white veranda with the rickety porch swing and frowning gargoyle of the god of the wind.

Sheryl watched her Uncle Fergus get out of the car, then the passenger door opened and out stepped a young man. He carried a guitar and stood nodding his head like one of those little crushed-velvet dogs in the back windows of cars. He was blond and willowy. He had a red bandana tied around his neck, worn the way cowboys did in Westerns. He took it off and mopped his face as if surveying the future writ large in the landscape in front of him.

Dr. Beat introduced a gospel tune by Ray Charles, *the brother who touches all our hearts*, who was blind, and therefore in Sheryl's mind, somehow closer to God. The background singers broke into a harmony that sounded like a heavenly choir, and Sheryl-Anne thought to herself that she was dreaming, surely she was daydreaming again.

Through the binoculars she could see the boy looking around, smiling and showing all his teeth in a grin that said he couldn't believe his good fortune. Sheryl saw the valley too for a moment through his eyes: the purple-singed hills and the blue craggy face of the escarpment, the green-drenched orchards and the silent trees in orderly rows like obedient children lining up outside in the schoolyard.

He moved, walking over to the front window of the Bonneville and then a strange thing happened. He leaned a shoulder onto the hot car, and the sun tilted off the chrome and showered his golden head with a sudden blinding metallic halo. Sheryl felt her heart beat in her throat. A wind came up, sneaking through the collar and arm holes of his white shirt and filled the cloth like a sail, and the sleeves billowed with light behind him. In a moment he moved away and was just a boy again but she already knew that everything was about to change in her life. And she got down from her perch and flew down the hill like the wind to meet him.

Peter Angelo, this here is our niece, Sheryl-Anne, her Uncle Fergus said introducing her, and the young man grinned.

Sheryl stared at him, her dark head cocked to one side, one hand idly scratching a mosquito bite. He had a small girl's nose, thick dirty-blond hair, a little bit of stubble on his chin. He was older than Sheryl, but he wasn't too tall and still boyish looking. His eyes were hazel with little flecks like small blue fish swimming in them. At first glance he looked a bit rough, but then he smiled and his face lit up and he was beautiful.

Pete here was just hitchhiking to Toronto when I gave him a lift, her uncle said. Looks like he's going to stay with us for a few days, maybe help out a little.

Sheryl stood drawing circles with the toe of her sneaker in the dirt. Something was not quite right. It was too quiet, and all at once she knew why. Their dog Lupus was silent. On any other day he would be hoarse by now, but there was nothing. No barking. No rustle of the chain.

The screen door whined and Sheryl's Auntie Eleanor called her in to help with dinner.

Nice to meet you, Sheryl said, and smiled shyly.

At supper later there were introductions all round, hands offered and shaken, names traded and repeated out loud, ample smiling with lots of teeth showing. In the kitchen Sheryl's Auntie Eleanor had laid out a big country spread with a ham casserole, *Paul Newman's favourite*, mashed potatoes with gravy, waxed beans and baby carrots. There were candles on the table and hors d'oeuvres like they had only at Christmas. Eleanor fussed about the kitchen, glamorous in a shiny blue shirtwaist, trilling, *Welcome, welcome, seat yourself,* in her special party voice, wiggling her hips and humming along to CFRB, bossing Sheryl around, who rolled her eyes but did as she was told, passing around a plate of little blocks of ham and pineapple on toothpicks, saying: *Cigars, cigarettes.*

Peter Angelo seated himself where Eleanor indicated and sat looking around the kitchen, taking in the yellow-flowered wallpaper, the sparkly silver faucets, the white counter and endless family photographs that checkered the walls.

At the head of the table sat Sheryl's uncle, Fergus MacRae, his hair jet black and Brylcreem slick, his large blue eyes magnified by coke-bottle glasses. He sat smoking, his hors d'oeuvres untouched, long lanky legs crossed.

Peter here is from Sault Ste. Marie where his father has an automobile repair business, Fergus said. He pronounced it, *otto-mow-beal,* making it sound like the Rolls-Royce of garages.

Peter nodded, a trifle bashful. He told them he had a mom and dad and a little brother named Anthony and a German shepherd. On weekends he fished Lake Superior and on weekdays he helped his Dad out in the garage.

I guess I can fix most anything under the hood of a car, he shrugged.

Sheryl stared hard at his hands, the long fingers lying inconspicuously on the good tablecloth, and was convinced they could work miracles.

I want you all to know we have a very talented youngster in the house, Fergus announced. Peter here is going to be a fine musician one day. I think we should celebrate, he added, ordering a beer for Peter who blushed and said, Thank you, sir, in a breathy shocked voice as if he couldn't believe his good luck.

Sheryl watched his beaming, sun-kissed face and swore she would marry him if he let her, in her mind they were already holding hands and hurrying down the drive.

Eleanor refreshed her cocktail with its miniature umbrella and brought the boy a beer, and they all clinked drinks across the table, Josh and Sheryl holding out their tumblers of milk.

Eleanor asked Sheryl to put on some dinner music. Sheryl was the official family disc jockey so she trotted happily into the living room, but stopped abruptly when she reached the doorway where the air shimmered in a veritable wall of heat, and she stood for a moment holding her hair off her damp neck. The room seemed suspended in time, painted with dust and fuchsia evening light. The picture window looked out onto the parched front lawn and she saw summer stretching out before her, full of new possibilities with a beautiful boy in the house. She had a headache from the heat and closed her eyes and when she opened them again she saw something stir on the lawn....

A mare stumbles over as though drunk in the hay. By the light of a kerosene lantern, two men tie her front hooves together and pull her back hooves apart, fastening them with rope to stall posts. The mare bellows and snorts, struggling, her eyes rolling about in the whites, huge with fear....

Sheryl pressed her small hands to her eyes until the sight went away. When she had recovered, she went to the glass and mercifully the horse was gone, there was only Lupus lying in his doghouse licking his dirty front paws. It had happened twice now in only one day. She calmed herself by remembering what her Uncle Fergus had told her. It's only pictures, he had said, just the mind running wild, kiddo. Maybe it was all the excitement of the day.

She looked around. The house was a maze of faded floral walls untouched since the forties. Off to one corner was a standup hi-fi with records stored in a built-in cupboard below, and she got out a stack of 45s starting with "Hello, Dolly!" and positioned the arm for continual play.

Back in the kitchen, Eleanor was talking with Peter in her flirty party voice, her cream-puff beehive bobbing.

Fergus is the town druggist, he works at Wallcott's Drugs. He's one of the most important people in town now, you know. He went to pharmacology college in Toronto and did his internship there, and then Mr. Walcott hired him on when it was over, just a few months ago. It's hard to find regular employment ... her sentence petered out, heavy with blame and disappointment.

Yes, I was a wanderer in the desert of the soul for a long time, Fergus said philosophically, but I'm home to stay. The MacRaes have been in this part of the country for generations now. My great grandfather came here for free land for the working. He sent his whole family, wife and ten children, to Cedar Hollow from up north in two boxcars with all their belongings, farm equipment and livestock, which consisted of twenty-three cattle, a sow, two horses and a dog.

They had a little collie named Woebegone, Sheryl added.

That's my girl, Fergus said and Sheryl smiled proudly.

Fergus reached into the black medical bag at his feet and pulled out a bottle of pills and took one capsule with water, smiling at the guest and saying, Hay fever. It's why I didn't go into farming.

My grandfather and my father after him had pigs, chickens and cattle, Fergus continued with his story, lighting up another cigarette. Until one day the local marketing man gave my father some advice. He said: Arter, you never make money from anyting dat eats.

Fergus chuckled. We've specialized in apples ever since, kiddo. Tending to the fruits of Eve.

Say something in Italian for us, Josh interrupted, but Peter protested he didn't speak Italian, he was Canadian like everybody else, his mother was Irish.

Irish! Fergus and Eleanor sang out in unison, relieved, and Sheryl thought Peter got better with every passing minute.

My Mom used to work at Pearl's Beauty Parlour in Toronto, Josh said, but there was no one named Pearl there.

Yes, Eleanor smiled, I was the main colorist.

The screen door slammed and Fergus's younger brother Eammon entered the room, wearing a T-shirt, a pack of Exports rolled into a sleeve. He had a troubled handsome face, the MacRae raven hair, but when he opened his mouth there was a gaping hollow where his two front teeth had been. Everyone said that he had lost them in a barroom brawl over a woman, but he had never confirmed this. Eammon helped himself to casserole in whopping spoonfuls and then stood leaning against the sink, eating noisily.

Eleanor introduced Peter as their handsome young guest and gave him a wink, flirting again, and Sheryl stared daggers at the older woman. Eleanor explained that there were three MacRae brothers: Earl and Fergus and Eammon. Fergus worked in town while Earl and Eammon took care of the orchard, she said. Although Earl had just built an abattoir across the road with his buddy Jimmy Garrick.

How do you do? Peter offered, but Eammon ignored him and went on to talk farm business with Fergus. He'd planted Cortlands all week, finishing only today. The last fifteen acres were now all new dwarf root stock, Eammon said, picking up a piece of bread and folding it whole into the damp hollow of his mouth.

Fergus turned to the guest, That's progress for you. This year we're planting little trees, dwarf trees no bigger than a man, that can cut picking time and production costs in half.

Eammon snorted, I just do what the boss tells me. Beats running up and down a ladder all day.

Fergus smiled and declared it was a fabulous time to be in farming. In a few years, science would have a remedy for every pest.

Sheryl thought of Eden Valley's infamous orchards with their large standard trees and luxurious green canopies. In comparison, the dwarf seedlings looked pathetic and spindly.

Turning to Eammon, Fergus asked if he had a job for their new house guest. Eammon sighed, clearly irritated, but said he'd speak to Earl. There was a lull in the conversation.

Mrs. Johnson is down with the cancer, Eammon said.

Terrible scourge, Fergus nodded. One day there'll be a cure for that too.

Still no sign of that missing McDonald boy, neither, Eammon added.

Shame, Fergus said.

Well, no rest for the wicked, Eammon concluded, excusing himself, the screen door slamming behind him.

Sheryl's aunt and uncle fussed over Peter, asking him if he'd had enough to eat, offering him another beer. When he said yes to the latter Sheryl and Joshua fought over who would go until Sheryl pinched her cousin and won. The fan whirred overhead. Their shirts were damp under the armpits.

Fergus pushed his meal away, having barely touched a morsel, and adjusting his glasses, he squashed his cigarette in the ashtray.

So, kiddo, Fergus said to Peter, tell everyone all about yourself.

Peter put down his fork and told them he had plans to become a folk singer, play guitar, travel the road. His folks had said he was a dreamer and a layabout, but that was the thing he wanted most. He'd run out of cash when Fergus picked him up and offered him a job so he was grateful for work. He looked up at Fergus with awe and Sheryl understood. For when he wanted to her uncle could make a person feel like the only one in a crowded room.

My Uncle Fergus helps a lot of people, Sheryl said proudly.

He's a photographer, Josh added.

Maybe you'll be famous one day too, Sheryl told Peter, and I can come to your sing-alongs.

Peter shrugged noncommittally, bashful again. I suppose, maybe. He took a swig of his beer and said that in Toronto they had cafes and bars with little red tablecloths, where people sat around and drank coffee and played guitar. Yorkville was where it was at. The drink seemed to have loosened his tongue and he slurred a little.

Shangri-la! Fergus declared, his eyes shining blackly in the yellow kitchen. Landing here you're halfway there, kiddo, he said, we'll take you when the apples are all in. Music is the language of the heart. I hope you'll find the faith and encouragement here you need to foster your singular talent.

Yes, sir, thank you, sir, Peter nodded.

Here's to new friends, Fergus said, holding up his drink, and everyone toasted Peter again while he grinned from ear to ear.

After dinner Sheryl's Uncle Fergus asked her to take the guest on a tour of the farm, so she took Peter through the barn, pointing out the old Ford tractor and the big nine-foot mower, the orchard trailer and sprayer and grader sitting like hulking ghosts in the summer heat. She showed him her rabbit room, leading him along the row of cages introducing him to the Netherland Dwarfs, Mop Lops and Mini Rexes with movie star names: Greta Garbo and Vivian Leigh, Grace Kelly and Clark Gable, thrilled to have a guest interrupt the lonely monotony of her days. She even offered to let him hold one of the rabbits, but Peter just shrugged and said, no thanks, unimpressed.

They drifted back outside to stare at the white dog, part wolf, part hound, short-haired and lean, with his oddly powerful upper body and his crippled hind feet. The dog watched them with cool blue marbles for eyes. He growled and the sound was chilling.

She told the hitchhiker the story of how she had gotten him as a gift when he was a puppy only three summers ago while they were at the farm visiting her grandmother. Lupus had been hit by a truck that August, and his hind legs were paralyzed afterwards. That's why they stuck up in the air like that, she explained. He had bitten her Uncle Fergus so they were forbidden to pet him, and Lupus had been tied up in the old riding ring ever since. Over the last while he had grown vicious, Sheryl told Peter. They stood watching the white mongrel, dusk creeping over the escarpment, mosquitoes whining in the grass at their feet.

We used to have a horse too, Sheryl added.

There was still time before bed so Sheryl showed Peter her secret place in the hayloft, where she'd constructed a small fortress out of old bales. She produced a tin can and a crumpled Rothmans package.

Don't tell nobody, she said, offering him a cigarette and he smiled wickedly. I always have a puff up here at night after feeding the rabbits.

They sat in the hay smoking, dust motes drifting in the fading light from the window above their heads, while Sheryl looked at him and pretended not to look. She figured he was a runaway like that McDonald boy who had disappeared.

Her Uncle Fergus often played the good Samaritan, picking up lost souls, hitchhikers and strays and bringing them to the farm for a night or two that became weeks and months. Most of them turned out to be layabouts who ate too much and stayed too long, before they were dropped at the roadside or voluntarily left town. This boy was different somehow.

So do you ever have dreams? she asked him, trying to wipe that bored look from his face.

Nah, he said, well, sometimes, I guess I don't remember them.

I do. Usually they're in black-and-white, but every once in a while, there will be something in colour. Like a colouring book where the kid only filled in the lawn green or the apple red, she said.

Black-and-white like television? he snorted.

I guess. My Uncle Fergus told me I have so many dreams because I have the *sight*.

The sight? he asked.

Yeah, you know, pictures in your head. Dreams of things before they happen.

Cool, he said and blew a smoke ring. He was quiet for a moment as though thinking on all this.

So, he said, if Fergus is your uncle, where's your parents?

She told him she wasn't sure, her mother had left her with her grandparents when she was only three. Sheryl had watched while her mother lifted a gloved hand and waved goodbye, then slipped into a blue car and disappeared down the drive.

Her Uncle Fergus told Sheryl her mother worked as an airline stewardess and a model. She had been Miss Home Hardware when she was a teenager. Sheryl had never met her daddy and she didn't care to. She told Peter that her mother was planning to send for her soon as she got more settled. She sent letters every month. Sheryl was waiting for the day when she turned sixteen then she was going to go live with her mother in Toronto. I'd walk out of here right now if I had someone to go with me, she said.

That so, Peter answered, taking the cigarette back again.

Sheryl said her mother was going to buy a big house with a white picket fence and a gold door knocker with a horse's head on it. And although this was a lie and she knew lying was a sin, the house was one of those things she had wished for for so long, the story felt like it was true and just flew out of her mouth before she could think better of it.

Sheryl had lived for a long time with her Uncle Fergus and Auntie Eleanor, who were kind enough to take her in after her grandmother died. She told Peter her uncle was like a father to her. Before he went back to school, they had been in one town after another, Elora and Sudbury and Hamilton and Toronto, and just about every place in between, Fergus being a Renaissance man and all.

What's that? Peter asked, and Sheryl shrugged. She wasn't sure but she thought it was someone who found it hard to stay put. She had come to the farm every summer when her grandparents were alive, but they had been back here in Eden Valley for a year now since her uncle got the job at the pharmacy.

She changed the subject to ask him if he had a favourite song and had he heard of The Supremes and, by the way, did he have a girlfriend where he came from?

You sure ask a lot of questions, he snickered. Peter took a puff of the cigarette and let the smoke curl outside his nostrils. They sat watching the light fade, blowing smoke rings. He seemed like an ordinary boy, preoccupied and moody and not easy to talk to, and Sheryl wondered about her vision from the lookout. Her Auntie Eleanor was forever telling her she was imagining things.

Monday morning, Uncle Earl came over to show Peter Angelo the ropes. Sheryl was dunking Cheerios, watching the rabbits on the bottom of her bowl cavort, wondering who ever thought of rabbits wearing dresses anyhow. She sat across from Peter who ate scrambled eggs with his mouth open, while Josh ran his toy truck through a puddle of spilt milk on the yellow vinyl tablecloth.

Well, if it isn't Mary, Mary quite contrary, Earl said, giving Sheryl a wink, coming into the kitchen, taking off his cap and smoothing back his thinning grey hair.

Earl is Fergus's older brother, Eleanor said by way of explanation to Peter.

Earl helped himself to coffee, chuckling, Yep, got a phone call at seven this morning from Fergus saying he'd picked up a hitchhiker on the highway, did I have a job for him.

Earl shook his balding head from side to side and chuckled. I don't know how he does it. The guy's a magnet for kids. Teenagers, Earl scolded, looking at Sheryl, I don't trust em. They're too smart for their own good. They have a rebel streak in them at least five years long. Isn't that right, Mary? he teased.

Sheryl studied the dressed-up bunnies and said nothing. Her Uncle Earl was always calling her funny names.

Josh said, I'm not a teenager.

Of course, you're not, darling, Eleanor said, rubbing his carrot-coloured brushcut with painted fingernails. Sheryl rolled her eyes at Peter.

Earl settled himself at the table and took a sip of coffee. He was so close Sheryl could smell him, he stank of the abattoir, a ripe animal stench that reminded her of cows and pigs, piss and fear.

Looks like another scorcher, Eleanor said, fanning herself with her magazine. She told Peter that Earl lived in the bungalow across the road, beyond the abattoir he had built with his friend Jimmy.

Uncle Earl has a lawn like a golf course, Josh boasted.

I'll be damned if there wasn't a clump of dandelions on it this morning. Lordy. Swear I sprayed every godforsaken inch of that sucker with D.D.T. There's not an insect with sense will alight on it, Earl sighed.

Eleanor gathered up her cigarettes and magazine and excused herself, her furry high-heeled slippers clicking daintily out the door.

So, lookin' for work, are ya? Earl asked.

Yes, sir, Peter said.

Well, I think we can arrange that.

The boy nodded, chewing.

Sheryl gave up on her Cheerios and padded about the kitchen making herself useful, her blue seersucker shorts making a crisp no-nonsense sound as she walked. She gathered the dishes, while Josh talked to his dinky toy at the table.

Where's your mother think you are now, son? Earl asked, suddenly.

Sheryl shut the water off and wiped the plates noiselessly, eavesdropping over the tap with its thin drip, drip, dripping into the dirty dishwater.

Toronto, she heard Peter say, his voice cracking nervously. Told everyone I was going to look for work.

Really? Earl returned, unconvinced. Was that in person or in a letter you left on the kitchen table? I bet she's worried sick about you. Probably got half the RCMP in the province of Ontario out looking for your hitchhiking ass.

Sheryl turned around and saw Peter put down his toast and slowly wipe his mouth with the back of his hand. She held her breath. The fan was whirring overhead.

Sir? he asked.

Don't sir me, the older man said. I just want to know what we're gonna say to the cops when they come knockin' on our door lookin' for ya.

I'm nineteen, Peter blurted out, in a couple of weeks, he added.

Sheryl bit her lip.

So why did you run away?

My old man, Peter said, studying his empty plate.

Did he throw you around?

Sometimes, Peter said, memorizing the vinyl tablecloth. Mostly my mother, he mumbled. He broke her arm.

He glanced up at Sheryl and looked away. She scratched at a mosquito bite on the back of her leg with her bare foot. She saw the endless stretch of highway, the hot sun on asphalt, Peter hitchhiking alone. If Earl sent him away it would be another long dreary summer.

Well, I'm glad we got that straight, Earl said. He told the boy finally that if the cops came he would have to leave but in the meantime Peter was to tell everybody he was a distant cousin helping out for the summer.

And this conversation never took place, or you're out on your ear, Earl warned.

Yes, sir, Peter said, sounding relieved.

Sheryl sighed and went back to the dishes.

Earl stayed at the table studying Peter. I'll be damned if you don't look like somebody. He snapped his fingers and turned to Sheryl. Slim, who does Peter here look like? What's the name of that dead kid, movie star, what was his name?

Jimmy Dean, Sheryl grinned, grateful for the change in conversation.

Yes, quite a resemblance to Jimmy Dean in that rebel movie. Pretty as a girl, Earl chuckled. Lord help you.

Every week day after that Sheryl awakened to the screen door slamming, as Peter and Eammon rose early and blundered out into the dawn while the sun was still opening its eyes and a lone cardinal carried on in the cedars. Sometimes Sheryl crouched by the window and watched them heading out to spray the fruit trees before the wind got up. Eden Valley's apple farmers sprayed early in summer as part of a regular regime in the endless battle against the apple's minuscule but multifarious enemies including moths, aphids, mites and sooty blotch, not to mention apple scab, the creepiest sounding of them all.

The chemicals needed to keep these pests at bay could win a war, her Uncle Earl always joked. Sheryl loved their names. They reminded her of the medicines in the jars at Walcott's Drugs. Latin names, foreign and diabolical sounding: Captan, Cyprex, Phygon, Parathion, D.D.T.

They arrived in big lumpy sacks like potatoes and were mixed in the old John Bean orchard sprayer then applied religiously in spring and early summer, especially when the weather was damp. Sometimes the sound of sprayers echoed like an air raid in the valley all day long. Paradise took a lot of work to maintain it seemed.

There had been a few hot damp days and the agriculture department issued a statement saying secondary scab infection was taking hold in the orchards. The fungus spawned in dampness, spreading a measly rash that meant death to the fancy apple. Eammon and Peter headed out especially early the next morning, the big V8 tractor guzzling gas and rumbling through the yard.

By the time Sheryl finished feeding the rabbits everyone had gone. The men were at work, Eleanor was over at Earl's giving his wife April a Toni, and Josh was playing with Andrew Vanderboch next door. The hall clock struck eleven and Sheryl startled at the gonging. She padded the deserted floors, wandering in and out of the hot empty rooms with nothing to do. In the kitchen, she stuck her head in the freezer to cool, ate half a box of chocolate chip cookies just because she could. She trolled upstairs and tried on all of Eleanor's slingback shoes, her barely-beige lipstick and false eyelashes, *Are they real or an eye-lusion?* and leafed through *The Hairpiece Stylebook*.

Tired of snooping, she trundled back to her room, collapsed onto her bed and lay listening to the radio, losing herself in daydream, the long-lost Valiant, coming up the drive, the prodigal mother dressed like a stewardess in a sky blue suit, the wide-open welcoming arms, followed by the predictable, *My how you've grown!!* There would be a trunk full of presents, lots of I'm sorry's, maybe her very own dog. Sheryl would look into her mother's face and finally know who she was, where she came from.

Soon her make-believe was interrupted by the news. Three civil rights activists were missing in Mississippi, a place she knew of only from spelling bees.

At noon, her Uncle Fergus came home for lunch, arriving out of the blue wearing his long thick white coat starched and official looking, buttons shiny, the sweat trickling down his temples. Sheryl picked at her shoe laces, feeling shy and awkward when she was alone with him, awestruck next to Fergus the great pharmacist, the second most important person in town after Doc McBrearty. She stared at his hands, which were fine and manicured like a lady's.

Hey Slim, how's my girl? he asked. He said he'd forgotten his antihistamines. He looked tired, there were dark circles below his eyes and his skin was the colour of milk. They ate grilled cheese sandwiches together in the canary-coloured kitchen, listening to CFRB natter on in the background. Sheryl asked him what activists were and he said they were troublemakers and she asked if that's why they were missing, but he merely stared at her curiously as if he hadn't heard.

After lunch, while they still had a moment alone, he told her he had a few things of her mother's he wanted to give her, and she felt as if he had read her thoughts. He brought out a pile of old books, Nancy Drew mysteries, *The Hidden Staircase, The Bungalow Mystery, The Secret of Shadow Ranch* and others, and she chose the one with the phantom horse on the cover, which reminded her of the grey mare that haunted her dreams.

She ran her fingers along the inside cover where her young mother had scrawled *March 1952* and the name: *Miriam.* Then the tears started and she couldn't stop. She wished she wasn't such a cry baby, she was always blubbering over dead animals in the road.

Fergus patted her head with his large palm. There, there, he said.

He got out an old album with an auburn-haired siren on the cover in a strapless red dress and told her, You wouldn't know it but this lady is a grandmother two times over. Your mother was as beautiful as she is and one day, Slim, you'll be just like her.

At the close of the day, Peter Angelo appeared out of the trees, riding the John Bean mower up the small dirt-rutted road towards the house, maneuvering the steering wheel with one deft hand, the other riding his hip, cocky as you please, his Hillman's Hardware cap on backwards and a bandage on his sunburned nose. Sheryl and Eleanor were on the porch and they waved at him as he passed and Eleanor called out, You're all sunburnt. You look like an Injun, offering Peter Angelo a smile that made Sheryl's face hurt.

Peter made it to the house just as Fergus drove up and sent Sheryl inside for beer. She let the screen door slam behind her bare heels as she disappeared into the cool wallpapered refuge of the house. Eleanor hollering after her, Don't slam the door, sighing when it was too late.

Inside, Sheryl rummaged around in the fridge and stood at the kitchen window, rolling the icy beer bottles over her warm skin. There was the sound of a lawn mower somewhere in the valley, the smell of fresh cut grass on the wind. The county road glistened, an imaginary lake floating on it from the heat. She could see Eleanor outside lying on the wicker sofa, a cigarette in one hand, legs bare and crossed, brightly painted coral-coloured toenails, each one separated by a tuft of cotton. She was complaining, I keep telling her to shut the door properly but she doesn't listen to me, you know. She never listens to me, Eleanor sulked.

Sheryl opened the beers and let the bottle caps ding into the sink. *Snappa Cappa Red Cap,* she whispered. Her mother would never complain, never say bad things about her, never flirt with the hired help. She would call Sheryl *dear* like Mrs. McBrearty did in church.

Sheryl could see Lupus's big white head against the barn wall, watching Peter and Fergus with alert and swivelling ears.

In the living room, Sheryl turned on the hi-fi loud and put on a stack of LPs. In a moment, the record player burst into life, the amplified crackle followed by the LP slapping down. The music drifted out onto the porch as Sheryl backed out cradling the drinks, the screen door slamming to behind her.

You see what I mean? Eleanor clucked, disapprovingly. She crossed a slender leg and Sheryl watched as Peter's roving eye followed the movement of Eleanor's near-naked calf.

Boys, Sheryl thought. A mosquito whined in the air. Somewhere off in the distance they could hear Josh blowing up his dinky toys again. Sheryl trotted across the porch barefoot and gave Fergus and Peter their beers.

There was a click as the record player fired up and Eleanor pulled the cotton from between her now dry toes, swung her legs off the couch and said, Come on up here Angelo and show a girl a good time. I need to practice my watusi.

And so Peter and Eleanor watusied on the porch, Eleanor gracefully twisting, her rosy dress flying up around her thighs, while Pete stumbled left-footed along, the two of them twisting and laughing. Fergus dashing in to get the Eastman Kodak and returning to take snapshot after snapshot, shouting: Smile, say cheese! Put your arm around Eleanor there, Pete, don't be shy-now there's a shot, while Sheryl's face sank beneath the cover of her Nancy Drew.

But when the first song was finished and another record had slapped down, Fergus told Peter to ask Sheryl to dance and she wrinkled her nose but her uncle shouted, Don't take no for an answer, young Pete. Soon they were all on the porch, Eleanor and Fergus and Sheryl and Peter, twisting and shouting.

That Saturday afternoon they went to the beach. Sheryl put on cat's eye sunglasses and pedal-pushers, her new pink polka-dot bikini hidden beneath. In Eleanor's bathroom she found a tube of Rue de la Pink lipstick and smeared it on her lips, making kissy faces in the mirror, then wiped the lipstick off but pocketed the tube all the same. In her room she stashed la Pink in her pencil jar under the picture of Northern Dancer, Canada's first Kentucky Derby winner. She kissed the horse, the fastest, most beautiful bay in the whole world, leaving a faint imprint on the horse's photographed flank, pressing her cheek against the picture, arms outstretched, pretending it was Peter.

Outside, the sky was an untroubled blue. The Pontiac looked brand new, transformed by soap and polish and sunlight and seemed to float along the country road, smelling of Armor All and fuel, the silver chrome of the car, reflecting back a shiny new world. Fergus played the good neighbour, waving at Vanderboch, the old Dutch gentleman who lived next door, as they pulled out of the drive. Through Sheryl's cat's eye sunglasses Eden Valley was tinted rose. The convertible top was down, they were bathed in summer light and their hair shone in rainbow highlights. They played I Spy with my Little Eye and sang "Ninety-Nine Bottles of Beer on the Wall" and Sheryl and Josh didn't fight once. In town, a billboard showed a Coke bottle and a smiling girl and underneath them both was written: **Things go better with Coke!** Joshua and Sheryl sang out in unison: *Life is much more fun when you're refreshed!* and everyone laughed.

Fergus fussed with the dials on the polished mahogany console, flipping through blips of troubling news: the U.S. was sending more troops to Vietnam, an off-duty police officer had killed a fifteen-year-old Negro boy. Then Fergus found Nat King Cole, and the news bulletins were forgotten and Nat was singing, "Those Lazy, Hazy, Crazy Days of Summer," and the children sang along. Once when they took a corner hard, Sheryl's small hand touched Peter's. He didn't pull away and a thrill shot through her. Hey, maybe there'll be someone wearing a topless bikini, Josh mused out loud.

In your dreams, Sheryl quipped.

At the lake they parked the tan Bonneville on the edge of the sand and Fergus had everyone pose beside the car, setting each person where and how he wanted them: Eleanor with hat, Pete between Josh and Sheryl, click, click, click, the whole family linking arms and showing their teeth, saying *macaroni and cheeeeese!*

They scooped a place on the beach already packed with warm bodies: teenage girls sun-tanning, dads barbecuing under the cedars, families with radios and lawn chairs, all staring out at the water in silent summer homage. A raft floated gently out on the lake, and children dove off it, the squealing and splashing sounds washing back onto shore in waves.

Eleanor lay on a chaise lounge, oiled and reeking of coconuts, while Sheryl's pale-skinned uncle parked himself under the umbrella with a book.

Get me a Coca-Cola from the cooler, won't you, darling? Eleanor said, eyes closed, hand held out. When Fergus had gone back to his chair, Sheryl saw Eleanor spike the Coke with a small flask and take a long swig.

Joshua dropped his shorts and ran to the water, diving in shirt and all, while Peter lazily took off his shoes and socks. Fergus had offered him a cigarette at the dinner table the other night and he lit up now, boldly smoking everywhere he went like an adult. He ran a hand through glossy hair, worldly in black sunglasses. His eyes roving the beach, arrested here and there by a bikini, a set of white shorts strolling.

Sheryl inched her towel forward as close as she could get to him, until she could smell his suntanned skin, the delicious smells of Coppertone, Juicy Fruit, and cigarettes. Shimmying out of her pedal-pushers and arranging her long, leggy body face down on the sand to read *The Secret of Shadow Ranch*.

Nancy was at a ranch in Phoenix, Arizona, haunted by a phantom horse and each time the horse appeared something bad happened, things went missing, someone got hurt, as if the horse was trying to tell them something. Sheryl caressed the image of the white animal on the cover. She envied Nancy Drew. Even though she was just a character in a book, the young sleuth had a car and could go anywhere and do anything, she was plucky and smart, beautiful and good. Sheryl would like to be a spy, a detective, a solver of mysteries. She lifted her binoculars, playing detective, zooming in on two little girls diving off the raft, appearing so close Sheryl felt she could whisper into their ears: *Watch out!*

The day was hot and dreamy. Sheryl found it hard to concentrate on things, the outlines of objects blurry in the heat. She trained her binoculars on Peter, examining his pores, the freckles on his shoulders. Peter sat like Mohammed, his shirt draped over his head and spilling down his back. Girls kept turning to stare at him and he would smile and wave back, silly and beautiful all at once with his headdress and sunburned arms, his sly half-smile. No matter how close she zoomed in on him, he was flawless.

Eventually the sun and water had an effect and Sheryl became too tired to read, her lids heavy from the heat, the waves lulling her to sleep. She closed her eyes just for a minute....

It is cramped and cold and smells like an outhouse, insects crawl in the dark under her naked skin, where the little girl lies shivering, afraid to move or breathe, having exhausted herself with shrieking. She is afraid they have left her to die, will forget her in this horrid place until the trap door opens, but they do not let her out, instead they throw something in. Something large and dank and slimy, that lands with a thud on her belly. She lifts a hand to touch it and feels the velvet muzzle, the coarse animal hair and her terror rises so huge it suffocates her screams....

Sheryl's eyes opened and she saw Peter peering down at her, skull-like with his black sunglasses and white headdress, and she gasped, leaping to her feet, yelling: Get it off me, get it off! slapping at invisible sand fleas.

Josh stood dripping wet on the sand, watching. There she goes again, having another hairy fit, he said. Then he turned to Peter and shrugged, Slim's crazy, she can't help it.

Pipe down over there, Fergus hollered, can't we have some peace?

There was a ship went down out there a long time ago and the hull is resting somewhere on the bottom, Sheryl said later to Peter. She had returned from a swim and sat swaddled in a towel, staring out at the blue eye of Boar's Head Bay, wondering how the water could look so beautiful and serene on the surface, while the bottom was littered with the old bones of drowned sailors and sunken ships, and the winter coats of ice fishermen who fell in every spring.

People say sometimes when the water's low you can see the mast rising out of the deep while you're snorkeling, but I think that's a story. Probably the ship just sits there on the sand, and everyone boats and fishes and swims overtop without ever once seeing it, she said to him.

The teenagers sat pondering the mysterious white-rimmed shore.

Yeah, Peter answered, people are blind.

Fergus took the leisurely route home, seeing as it was such a glorious day, and Sheryl sat in the back seat letting the wind buffet her face, as they drove through the quiet town of Cedar Hollow with its wide streets lined with elms, maples and cedars. They stopped at a roadside stand where white-haired twins sold lemonade for a nickel a glass. The family got out of the car and stood leaning against the Pontiac squinting in the sun, slapping away flies, drinking the cool sugary lemonade.

On the way through town, they dropped in at Walcott's Drugs, the sign in the window: *Silverwoods Ice Cream Sold Here*. Sheryl walked up the aisle, Josh at her side, tall rosewood cabinets reaching from floor to ceiling on either side with precious glass cases and mysterious nameless bottles on the shelves. There was the tap-tap-tap of the typewriter in the back as someone typed out a prescription, the phone rang, the atmosphere was library-serious and medicinal, that squeaky clean dentist smell everywhere. Mrs. Walcott came out from the dispensary in the back, taking her glasses off her nose and holding out her hand to shake Uncle Fergus's, her hair in a strict bun, her glasses resting on a string on her large bosom, which jiggled as Fergus joked with her, introducing her to all of them.

So this is where I work, kiddo, Fergus said to Peter, when Mrs. Walcott had gone to help a customer. Finest drug store for miles, son, the future's in pharmaceuticals.

Peter nodded. Cool.

Fergus showed them around, pointing out the long white hidden counter where the drugs were kept, the compounding room where the prescriptions were filled out in code. He spoke in a hushed respectful voice while Mr. Walcott peered at them all above his lowered glasses with suspicious eyes, small moustache twitching, humourless on his imperious raised platform with its glass walls and arsenal of powders and ointments and shelf upon shelf of mysterious concoctions in little boxes, elixirs and potions with names Sheryl couldn't pronounce.

The prescriptions are all written in Latin, Sheryl whispered to Peter. My Uncle Fergus learned Latin in pharmacology college, she boasted and Peter nodded and said Cool for the hundredth time.

Fergus talked to a customer with a kindly bedside manner. Well, hello there Mrs. Darling, how's the arthritis? he said, his conversation periodically drowned out by the ringing of the door chimes, as children bored with endless summer came in to peruse the ballpoint pens and paper notebooks, and housewives in flowered dresses wandered the aisles in search of Milk of Magnesia and nail polish.

My, my you've done well for yourself, Fergus, Mrs. Darling said. We're all proud of you.

Yes, well I'm a certified pharmacist now and delighted to be working here at Walcott's Drugs, Fergus smiled.

Marvellous, Mrs. Darling chuckled pleasantly, and moved on.

After they'd paid their respects to Mr. Walcott they slipped next door to The Little Apple Dairy Bar, and the children sat in a red vinyl corner booth and ordered root beer floats. Peter asked for black coffee and pulled out a candy bar, not bothering to take his shades off and sat there looking like a movie star, T-shirt sleeves rolled up, head back, hair sticking up wild from the wind, doing imaginary drum rolls with his fingers on the grey Arborite. Sheryl didn't take her glasses off either, the dairy bar pink-stained and shadowy behind her sequined cat's-eyes, and sat slurping through her straw hoping people would think they were boyfriend and girlfriend.

Mrs. Harvey came to take their order. Josh sat next to Sheryl fidgeting and entertaining himself by hopping up and down on the cushioned seat, which made farting noises when he sat on it abruptly. He kept turning to everyone saying, Who did that? Was that you? Oh, Sheryl, pulease, not silent but still deadly! until Sheryl told him to grow up and Eleanor blew smoke from her glossy lips and said, Stop picking on him, he's only a kid.

There were miniature juke boxes at the tables, and Sheryl rifled through the plasticized lists of top-ten songs, pleading with Eleanor for a quarter to play something, until her auntie gave in and slid one across the table to Sheryl, saying, Honestly, Slim, sipping her coffee from a white porcelain cup and leaving it rimmed with peach lipstick.

The Supremes came on, and they sat staring into their floats, Peter humming along, dunking his Baby Ruth bar into his coffee cup, the day growing weary and their enthusiasm waning with the afternoon while Motown battled with the British Invasion at the next table.

Back in the car, they drove home, through the summer oasis of Eden Valley, the cicadas whining in the hot sun, everyone quiet and drowsy. Sheryl unrolled the window all the way down, the countryside a blurring checkerboard through her half-closed eyes, her mind wandering. Josh spied a dead skunk by the side of the road and said, Pee you, did you ever notice how skunks smell like rubber?

Staring ahead, Sheryl was distracted by a figure, a scruffy boy sauntering by himself. He looked to be about her age and as the car drew closer, she saw that his clothes were mismatched and colourless as a hobo's, his hair dark brown, the colour of hide, sticking out every which way in furry tufts. He held a stick in his hand, a long crooked stick worn pale and smooth and ancient-looking by the water of Boar's Head Bay. Something about that boy, walking lonely by the side of the road, something about that stick drew Sheryl's eye and would not let go. She had seen him before but couldn't remember where or why.

Josh shouted, Hey, look who it is. Levon the moron. Turning to Peter he said, Watch this, and sticking his head out the window he made a coyote hooting noise, but the boy trudged on, oblivious.

Sheryl remembered him now.

Who's Levon? Peter asked, and Fergus answered.

He's a local deaf kid.

His father's an Indian, Josh said. A dead Indian.

Sad story, Fergus said, watching the boy on the road ahead. Lives with different relatives, not ever with one for very long.

He's retarded, Josh said.

He is not, Sheryl said and she didn't know why she said it, because she wasn't really sure whether he was or not, she just didn't want to agree with Josh. Besides she liked any kid like herself who didn't have a regular family. She knew bad things had a way of happening to people.

He just can't hear, she said. And it was true, even as they came upon him he didn't turn around at the noise of the approaching car and to prove the point Josh sang out the window: Levon's a moron, Levon's a moron, but his words floated lost and cruel on the wind, missing their target.

The boy didn't look up at all until the car ahead of them swooshed past, making a wind that moved his hair and threw dust into his eyes so that he was temporarily blinded. He stopped, startled by the intrusion and blinked. Sheryl watched as he saw the shiny vanilla Bonneville for the first time and registered her red-haired cousin leaning out the window insulting him, and she thought how strange it must be to see a mouth opening and closing and not hear a word, like watching television with the sound off. Levon's eyes alighted on her too and she was suddenly ashamed to be in the car. An expression of disappointment appeared on his serious face, and Sheryl knew that Levon understood Josh was making fun of him.

In the split second it took for them to pass one another, he looked at her. Sheryl sensed a kindred loneliness there that made her want to enter his deaf world, and hear the empty silence.

She saw that he had decorated his walking stick. A feather hung from the handle, secured with an old brown shoelace, and the feather was long and rust-coloured, but most startling of all was the eye. He had painted a bright blue eye with a red iris on the stick that was eerily familiar. She watched him grow small in the side mirror, where he walked on staring after them.

He isn't stupid, she said to Josh, he's just deaf.

Fergus also watched the boy in his rear-view mirror but said nothing.

Levon the moron, Josh chanted again, and Fergus chuckled and they flew off up the road leaving the boy and his cane far behind.

Fergus told them the story of Levon's father.

Indian Bob showed up one day in town with that boy trailing behind, snot nosed and deaf and barely a pair of shoes on him. Indian Bob hunted in the bush back then, lived in a shack he'd built himself down by the dump. He was an Aqua Velva man, Fergus joked. Runaway from that special Indian school.

One day he was found floating in three feet of water in the river, Fergus continued. That boy's been passed around from one relative to another ever since. Finally Apple Valley sent him to a school for deaf children in Milton a couple years back where he learned hand language. He's there most of the time now I believe, home only on holidays and some weekends.

Does he live with aunts and uncles? Sheryl asked. And Fergus replied that he might very well.

Sheryl put her hands over her ears for the rest of the way home. Her clammy palms blotted almost everything out, and for a brief moment she felt what it was to have the whole world inside her head, and it seemed familiar and safe to her that way, held at a proper distance, like a dream.

After dinner they took a stroll through the orchard under the cool green umbrella of summer trees, taking refuge from the day's heat. Fergus a dark stick figure ahead, striding through the long green twitch-grass leading the way. Peter hurried beside Fergus struggling to keep up, hanging onto Fergus's every word while Sheryl loitered behind feeling cranky and left out. Joshua was already dressed for bed in his cowboy pyjamas, and he followed Sheryl in his slippers, whining, *Wait up, wait up!*

Take a look around you, what you see here is the garden of Eden, Fergus said, extending an arm towards the trees. Sheryl looked but saw only bark and leaves, the bland unknowable face of nature, serene on the surface, ruthless and twisted at its roots. The orchard was cool now and quiet but for a bat that flew in and out of the trees with a kamikaze whirring and Josh and Sheryl ducked as it passed overhead.

Think of the fruit of the tree of knowledge, Fergus said, the serpent wound around its trunk, green foliage studded with ruby red apples. The ancients saw the Tree of Knowledge and the Tree of Life as the same. The whole story of Eve, Adam and the serpent in the tree was a misinterpretation of old paintings of the Goddess giving her devotees an apple-the gift of life. The Christians turned these symbols upside down and made them evil. The moral of this story, kiddo, Fergus winked, is that life is never as simple as it seems.

Starlight, star bright, first star I see tonight, I wish I may, I wish I might, be able to sleep through the whole darn night, Sheryl rhymed, snuggling in her window seat wearing rocking-horse pyjamas. She gazed up at the crescent moon and imagined the astronauts one day walking there, stepping across endless fields of white pockmarked space. Pondered the complexities of peeing without gravity. The night was a chorus of mating frogs, and the sky spiralled into a perilous black infinity.

She heard voices out on the porch, and realized Fergus and Peter were still outside drinking and talking. Bottles crashed in a noisy toast. Fergus went inside and his footsteps were lost momentarily in the house. From where she lay, her long limbs pretzelled, Sheryl could see Peter's worn Hush Puppies on the stairs, and her heart ached at the sight of them. She watched the violet plume of his cigarette smoke floating up from where he sat alone, dying to call out to him, *psst, up here,* like Juliet to Romeo, but Fergus soon reappeared and the porch light went on, banishing darkness to the yard.

There was shuffling and whispering. She could gather only bits and pieces of their conversation. A match was struck, and Sheryl watched their silhouettes reflected against the silent face of the barn wall, the tall man and the eager boy, their thin shadow hands passing something back and forth to one another.

Soon Peter's voice grew loud from the drink. He told a story about a Mercury GT he'd fixed and his father's dangerous drinking, described the fights and Saturday night beatings and how that same father cried on Sunday afternoons and begged forgiveness.

I'll never be like him, never, Peter slurred defiantly, knocking his beer over and for a moment Sheryl wondered if he was crying.

A puff of smoke billowed out into the yellow circle of porch light and a familiar scent drifted up to her window, smelling of nature wild and rooting, a sweet and sour odour that made Sheryl think of lawn mowers and scented underwear drawers and long troublesome nights. She wished Fergus wasn't turning him on, she knew her uncle meant to be friendly, hospitable, some said he was generous to a fault, but he had a way of corrupting people too. She blew on the windowpane and drew a heart in the mist of her own breath with Peter's initials and her own.

Choose me, she whispered, cradling her pillow that was somehow Peter and her mother and every heartache and longing she'd ever had all at once.

In the dream, the girl wears a beautiful dress, a long white dress with lace on the front.

On her cheek is painted a spiral. A wreath of woven daisies is placed upon her head. I am special, she thinks, counting out the years: One, two, three, four, five, six.

The girl walks along, stumbling under the heavy dress, plagued with dizziness, her steps gradually becoming slower until the earth slips beneath her feet, the sky belly flops and the grey trees spin. When she awakens she is lying somewhere else. The dress descends over her head like snow falling, the whiteness suffocating, the wind on her bare legs....

Sheryl awakened panting, afraid to move, skin swimming in sweaty sheets. Her hair was damp and stuck to her forehead in twisted ringlets. She could hear her own blood pulsing in her ears. That nameless night fear was loose and skulking in her room, the nightmare that turned chairs into leering faces and doorways into bogeymen. Her door was ajar and there was the faint smell of smoke in the room.

Outside the night was hot, dull and still, a thunderstorm brewed in the wings. Sheryl counted to a hundred then threw the damp sheet from her body and sat hugging her knees. She heard something: a staccato rhythm, low and insistent, like drumming or a heartbeat.

She crept to the window, telling herself she wasn't imagining the sound, her crazy mind wasn't making up things like Eleanor said, she could hear it plain as day. There was a light on in the barn. The night was full of sighing. Her skinny body ached from lack of sleep, she peered at the clock, only six hours again. She rested her chin on her knees and counted out six with her small fingers.

Then she saw them: fireflies. Like gentle aliens they hovered above the grass, sending out their tiny neon SOSs, silently bobbing in the damp heat. There was a clatter of thunder, and the fireflies scattered among the cedars.

The next time Sheryl awakened, daylight had crept into the room, and the house was quiet. She lay, watching the light steal onto things, stunned by how peaceful and safe the world seemed in daylight.

At the bureau she foraged for blouse and shorts catching a glimpse of her thin-hipped boyish frame in the mirror as she changed. Her breasts were small and hard and itchy as mosquito bites. She scratched at them and they ached.

The guest room where Peter was staying lay across the hallway. She tiptoed towards the forbidden door and knelt there, placing a small ear to the wood, smelling paint, varnish, dust. Crouching by the door handle she pressed her eye to the keyhole, and the little white dresser came into view, then the cupboard, then the cherry-wood bed with the four corner posts.

He lay on his belly with his face away from her, dirty hair tossed on the pillow. He clutched the sheet with one hand but had pulled the covers off himself and sprawled naked across the bed.

Later that morning they loitered outside Grace Anglican with the other church goers: young girls in white socks and gloves and crinolines, women with small hats pinned to their heads and men in summer suits, their hair parted so severely you could see the pink flesh of their skulls winking through. Standing stiffly in their Sunday best, they said hello to one another in quiet churchy tones.

A group of girls gave Sheryl the once over and she felt silly all of a sudden in the puffy blue gingham that Eleanor had bought for her, tottering in high heels, a bubble-knit cardigan thrown over her shoulders, her hands sweating in white kid gloves. The girls giggled, and Sheryl felt envious of their happy clique. They were girls who played bingo and went to the drive-in Saturday nights, while she knew no one outside her adopted family.

Peter was wearing a borrowed sports jacket and polished boots and his too-big-for-his-face sunglasses, and kept looking around nervously.

You look handsome, she whispered and he turned towards her, You don't look so bad yourself, Slim, and they stood for a moment smiling at each other.

Inside the church was hot as the pit of hell itself, a large fan whirring uselessly above, her hair summoned heavenward in its wind, flies shamelessly fornicating in the corners of windows.

The sermon was on *The Inevitability of Evil*, and the priest began by berating them for the wages of sin, warning them about the moral lassitude growing like apple scab in these turbulent times.

There was a symphony of creaking wood and coughing, the occasional eruption from an unhappy child. Sheryl sat squished between

Eleanor and Josh on the wooden pew, the wood lemon-scented and sticky. It was hard to think, that nervousness that afflicted her Sundays was suddenly everywhere, in the Bible windows, in the priest's cadence. Even the coughing seemed somehow unkind, malevolent, and she closed her eyes and drifted, thinking of Peter, until the priest's voice brought her abruptly back again.

Beware the darkness within!

Sheryl looked up and saw God with his fierce eyebrows and grey hair. God in his stained glass story with his army of airborne attendants judging and condemning. And it seemed as if God left off his business with Moses and the Ten Commandments to turn and glare at Sheryl-Anne MacRae, a pale teenaged not very good girl overheating in blue gingham. Suddenly it was all too much. Sheryl sighed and fell off the edge of the conscious world, her small body settling in a faint on the cool marble floor of Grace Church.

She awakened seconds later to Eleanor, hissing, Slim, get up. Her auntie yanking her back up onto the bench, slapping her wan face with a gloved hand, while the woman in the pew ahead barked, That girl needs airing.

It's too hot in here, Eleanor snapped back.

In the ladies' powder room, Sheryl bent over the faucet and drank and drank, then held her face under the cool water. When she was finished she stood up and saw Eleanor perched on the sink, staring.

Well, I hope you're pleased with yourself, she smirked.

That night Sheryl finished feeding her prized rabbits, stroking their long lop ears, topping the rattling tin containers with pellets, indulging them with alfalfa hay, lingering in the Cave of the Cottontail by the dim light from the single yellow bulb in the barn, when a shuffle in the other room gave her a start.

She felt that foreboding that came with dusk creepy crawling along the hairs on her arms, and she squeezed Greta, burying her face in the rabbit's butterscotch fur, whispering, You're my princess, hey?

Sheryl often felt strangely nervous at nights and on Sundays. With that nervousness came the voices, the pictures, the *sight*. The feeling even had a smell, like a windowless room full of sleeping bodies. She had that feeling now.

Watch out, the voice whispered.

Swallows scattered abruptly in the other room, Sheryl heard the footfalls again and pressed the Mini Rex to her. When she looked back Eammon loomed in the doorway, his long arms leaning on the mantle above, his skin sallow in the light. His eyes were feverish and watery from drink and he grinned. The Cave of the Cottontail shrank, suddenly stale and too small for the both of them.

I hate you, that small voice hissed inside her head, and it was so loud she worried he might hear it.

Slim, he slurred, how's my favourite girl?

Fine, thanks, she said feigning busyness.

Feeding the rabbits, are ya?

Just finishing, she said sweeping the table with a dirty hand, crunching the top of the burlap bag, gnarled hair falling forwards to cover her face. He stooped inside and leaned against the table beside her, so close now that she could smell the sweat of his clothes, the hot beery stink of his breath.

You're a good girl, Slim, he whispered, his face torn and broken, some inexplicable affliction there, and he reached out to tousle her hair, but Sheryl thrust the pedalling rabbit into his arms, saying breathlessly, Hold her for a minute will ya, I can hear the cat, then she bolted, the cedar door slamming behind her.

Outside, the sky was purple and the Hay moon hugged the horizon in a yellow haze, the way it did sometimes in July. The escarpment was midnight blue, the orchard serene, the trees hissing gently in the wind.

The porch was brightly lit, the whole family had come over for Sunday dinner as usual and they always retired to the porch afterwards in the good weather for drinks and dessert. The conversation rose in small waves, the laughter echoing in the yard, ice cubes in cocktail glasses clinking.

Sheryl sat on the porch steps beside Earl's skinny wife April, who smiled and asked, How you doing, kid?

Earl was in the midst of a story they all knew well, a piece of oat grass between his teeth, the end fluttering in the air.

Fergus was picking one day, Earl laughed, father had sent him up into the higher branches because he was light and nimble and did a good set—that's the way you set up your ladder against the tree there, Pete. And there he was like a bird way the hell up in God's country, it was the close of a day and there's good old dad below, always the slave driver, hollerin' up at him: *Hurry it up, hurry it up, I don't have all day.* Yellin' at Fergus when he rushed and dropped an apple or two. And Lordy, wouldn't you know it, on the horizon a storm starts brewing. Before you can say Jim Dandy, a wind comes up, and the sky is going all black and snarly, but before there's a drop of rain and young Fergus can get himself finished and back down that ladder, a stick of lightning comes out of nowhere, and in a blinding flash it whacks the tree. Pop's yellin' to beat the band, callin' for help, and Momma comes runnin' down from the main house, the tree is on fire and the wind is howlin' and her hair's all over hell's half-acre and she's bawlin' her eyes out, thinks she's done lost her favourite son. And here's Fergus cool as a cucumber coming down the ladder step by step and when he gets to the bottom he turns to Dad with his basket proudly and says: Didn't lose a one.

Here we thought he'd been hit, but the lightning never touched him.

Fergus sat quietly invincible, blue eyes beaming, long legs crossed, the cigarette going back and forth to his mouth, while all eyes turned to him in admiration.

Rubber boots, he laughed. I took it as a sign, he added mysteriously. I saw this blinding light, and at first I thought I'd died and gone to my maker. My life changed after that day. I always felt I was spared for a reason.

Sign? Sheryl said.

Amen, Earl said and his wife April echoed him. It was a thing they had started doing lately, ever since Peter arrived, saying Amen and Hallelujah like Fergus was a preacher or something, and they were all in church, but a church with guitars and cocktails and hootenannies out on the porch. Sheryl couldn't tell if they were joking or they were suddenly crazy for God but something was different. It had all started when they had come back to live on the farm, and while Fergus didn't have a job he had read a whole bunch of books, underlining and scribbling things in the margins and wandering the house saying, It's all making sense now, like he was in a trance or something. All of a sudden he started having a lot of ideas and talking about the coming of the new world and things began to happen just like he said they would. He had gotten a job at the pharmacy and bought the dwarf trees and organized Eammon and the orchard and even helped Earl buy the abattoir, and there was money now for things there never had been before when Fergus was in school and they all lived in a little flat in Toronto. It was hard now even to remember the dark and dingy days when they'd camped in windowless rental apartments, had macaroni and cheese for dinner every night and Sheryl's uncle had lain on the chesterfield for hours not talking.

The men sat on the porch now and yakked about how these were the good times, and they treated Fergus with the kind of respect you treat a doctor or a policeman. Fergus had always been the smart one, but now he seemed extra-special. Every day he was a bundle of energy and enthusiasm, and Sheryl was proud because he was like a father to her, the closest thing to a father she'd ever known.

What sign? Sheryl asked again, but nobody answered.

As I remember it, I still got a hiding for having taken so long, Fergus said.

You certainly had your share of beatings, Earl added, I don't know why, but Lordy, papa sure had it in for you.

Peter looked over at Fergus wide-eyed, and Fergus smiled.

Builds character, he cackled.

Josh said, Okay Pete, watch, I'm Sheryl when she sees a bee. He leapt off the stairs, his hands flapping up and down at his sides, squealing in a silly girlish falsetto, *Get it away from me, get it away,* running in loopy circles on the grass.

They all laughed.

Drop dead, Sheryl said, hugging her knees.

A hand-rolled cigarette appeared out of nowhere. Fergus passed the reefer to Peter who looked nervous, but Fergus calmed him, saying, Don't worry we're all family here. We share everything.

Peter took a drag of the cigarette and exhaled.

I had a dream not long ago that I lay in a circle, Fergus said, a white circle. I lay naked on an altar, stark naked with incense burning and candles, and there was a blinding light from above, and I saw a goat and a lamb. Suddenly I knew that the true law is man's will, what is evil often does good, and what is good sometimes turns for evil. And knowing this my heart opened, embracing everything, and I felt free

Fergus closed his eyes, and the porch was silent, all eyes watching him. Change is going to rise up like a great white dove and sweep the world. We're in the final process. In preparation we need to let go of the old game and embrace one another like one big family, kiddo, one big tribe. God is the Great Mathematician, he said; he seemed to be addressing everyone but his eyes were on Peter's.

In Genesis, God creates fruit after the land and sea but before the sun, the moon or Adam and Eve. Go forth, be fruitful and multiply, he tells us. The apple, *malus domestica* was in the beginning, in the garden of Eden. Why? Because the apple is the fruit of the gods, the nectar of Apollo and Aphrodite, and look at us—surrounded by apples for miles!

He pushed his glasses up his thin nose. I believe that Lee Harvey Oswald did not act alone, and the shooting of the American President last year was more than a shooting, it was a sign of things to come. Of the end of the old world.

Hallelujah, Eleanor said.

Lordy, Earl added.

Sheryl interrupted, I have dreams too ... but again no one paid any attention and she felt lost and invisible. Peter launched into a round of "This Land is Your Land" and a ragged trio of voices joined him in the chorus. When he was finished, the adults returned to talking among themselves about how the U.S. was sending more troops to Vietnam, the space program, the latest flag design, all the signs of the new world.

Inside the living room was an aquarium, and Sheryl and Josh swam in the cool underwater light of the TV. They had been sent in to watch television while the adults continued their party in peace.

Tonight we're going to have a really big sheyow, Ed Sullivan said and Josh spoke along with him in flawless imitation.

And now for the amazing, the thrilling, a treat I know you viewers at home are going to enjoy, please welcome... The television droned on, but Sheryl wasn't listening. The laughter outside erupted with a hilarity somehow chaotic and cruel. The light of the TV flickered on Josh's rapt face like pool water, menace lurking in the shadows of the blue room, in the predictability of the Sunday night ritual.

Sheryl pulled out a stack of old magazines and her scrapbook from under the coffee table.

There was the crackle and sulfur stench of a struck match, and through the window Sheryl could see Fergus lighting another reefer and passing it to Peter. Their smoking frightened her.

She flipped through her magazine, turning page after page of blondes and redheads until there she was in an advertisement for wigs, brown eyes roundly hopeful, dark hair in a Sassoon bob, beside her the words: *A little fakery these days means a whole lot of chic.*

Sheryl snipped carefully around the fashionable face, then cut out more pictures of grinning midnight-haired children, creating a perfect family for her scrapbook, like the ones she saw in commercials on TV. Good-looking families with obedient hair, who never lost jobs and travelled about, or picked up hitchhikers and did drugs on the porch, and she wondered who they were and where they came from and why she wasn't one of them.

The moon peered in, watching them, and goosebumps travelled her arms, the Sunday night feeling.

Josh mimicked the Mexican mouse, saying along with him: *Eddie, before I go to sleep, keeess me good night*, breaking into that silly Hispanic mouse giggle until Sheryl told him to shut up. The TV audience laughed in the hollow synchronized way they always did, and she gnawed on her thumb until she tasted blood. Suddenly terrified and lonely for her mother, for Peter, for some other life perhaps.

Eleanor entered briskly from outside, smelling of *l'Air du Temps* and vodka and gave Sheryl the drink she had sometimes to help her sleep.

Don't forget to pee before you go to bed, Sheryl said to Josh as they ascended the stairs, or you know what happens.

I can't help it, he whined.

I know, she said and hugged him.

It is the beginning of the end of the old world. The sky is grey, there are bolts of lightning and crackling thunder. The girl looks up and out of the sky they come riding, the four horsemen. Galloping forward, bringing war, plague, famine and death. The sun turns black as midnight and the moon glows red as blood, all the water in the rivers and lakes becomes a poisonous boil and the stars fall crashing to earth. The world cracks open like an egg and yolk spills, scorching everything it touches. The girl runs, heels burning, through this corroding black-and-white world. It will be Sunday night forever now.

The next day they walked dirge-like along the blacktop on their way to the variety store in town, dragging their feet, wrung out from the heat, a soggy unlikely trio: Sheryl and Joshua and Peter. Crickets and frogs sent up a chorus from the roadside ditches, tall pines on either side of the road cast long cool shadows in the dirt. The sun was high in the sky and painfully hot, searing the tops of shoulders, knees, noses and ears. This was already the second heat wave of summer, they'd had the hottest June in 124 years, and, worse, the weather man was predicting record temperatures for a few days more. Eammon and Peter had spent several long hot days planting another hundred dwarf trees, until mercifully Eammon had let him off early this afternoon.

They trudged along. Josh wore a baseball cap and a long-sleeved shirt and a Band-Aid on his nose, his freckled skin raw and peeling in places where he hadn't been so careful. Sheryl wore a straw sun hat, pedal-pushers and the cat's-eye glasses, her blue-black hair sticking to the sweat on the back of her neck.

Walking slowly, dragging their feet, they swatted at midges flying in cascading orbits before their eyes, their bodies waterlogged and tired. Peter hummed to himself and occasionally the wind rustled a leaf or two but even then brought little relief. Josh lagged behind, sloshing through the ditches on the sides of the road in his laceless running shoes. When they got out of sight of the house, he rose up out of the gully, hands in squirmy sunburnt fists, round eyes like glassy marbles, feverish.

Want to see what I got?

No, Sheryl said, not forgiving him for coming along, she had wanted to be with Peter alone. But Josh opened his fists anyhow and she and Peter gazed down on their vile contents: the torso of a frog in one and in the other, its severed legs.

Frog's legs, Josh giggled wickedly, his face red.

That's disgusting, Sheryl said and told him to put the frog out of its misery.

It's only a stupid frog, Josh protested, but he did what she told him all the same, smashing the head with a rock and tossing the body back into the water, hovering morosely over the ghoulish floating corpse, while Sheryl improvized a small prayer.

They turned and continued on their way in silence, lulled by the heat and cricket song, and Sheryl was so hot she felt her body floated along without her. It happened like that sometimes, she would feel as though her body was walking by itself, and she was somewhere else watching from afar. She wondered who that body belonged to, who she was.

She wiped the damp wiggly hair from her face and looked at Peter who was beautiful as always in his white shirt, dark blond hair and movie-star sunglasses. His beauty somehow transformed the walk, the day, the sad way life arranged itself in Sheryl's mind. He made her feel hopeful inside. Peter kicked at a pine cone and sent it rolling lumpily along the dirt road, bouncing over puddles and stones, a wobbly messenger of his thoughts.

I still think you look like Jimmy Dean, she said, smiling shyly at him, and he ran a hand through his hair, clearly pleased.

Yeah? he said, I guess I do. Well, I think you look a little like that girl, that skinny girl, eh, in My Fair Lady? I saw her in a picture somewheres, what's she called?

Audrey Hepburn, Sheryl said.

Yeah, her. Pretty but skinny with long arms and legs; he said this thoughtfully.

She does not look like a movie star, Josh sulked.

Sheryl told him to shut up and lifted her hair off her neck pretending it was short and said she wouldn't mind being Audrey Hepburn. A black fly landed on her arm and she slapped it away.

Well then, who do I look like? Josh said.

Like a goof, Sheryl said laughing, and Josh said, I know you are but what am I? and they stuck their tongues out at one another.

Peter interrupted them and said, I know—you look like that stand-up comedian, Red Skeleton. Yeah, that's it, Red Skeleton as a boy.

Josh shrieked with pleasure. *Good night and God bless*, he said in imitation, his head wagging from side to side, and they fell over themselves in the road giggling.

They headed out to County Road Ten, pretending to be their alter egos, Audrey and Red and Jimmy Dean out for a stroll, took a left and followed the back road that paralleled the highway into town wandering one of the many tree-lined and tree-named streets until they got to Wong's Variety.

Inside they loaded up on chocolate popsicles and red licorice to share, blackballs for Josh, Juicy Fruit gum and sweetheart candies for Sheryl, and Peter bought a Baby Ruth bar and a box of matches. They took their loot and drifted back out the door to sit on the white bench put there especially for loiterers like themselves.

When they licked their popsicles down to the sticks, Sheryl handed out the sweetheart candies, reading out loud the sickly sweet messages before she passed them on: *Be Mine, My Baby, Dear Heart*. Peter lit up a cigarette he'd hid in his pocket and Sheryl stole puffs. The afternoon droned on with the distant saw of lawn mowers, the stop and start of summer traffic, Peter pointing out the names and makes of cars as they came along, *Stingray, Mustang, El Dorado*, telling them how when he became a famous folk singer he was going to buy himself a white convertible Corvette with seats the colour of lipstick, and head out to the highway in that baby doing 130 miles an hour, radio blasting and the telephone poles flying past like they had wings on them.

You are so cool, Josh said, imitating him, and Sheryl was quiet for a moment fretting about that open highway and how Peter would disappear down it one day leaving them all behind. She wanted summer to never end, or for Peter to take her with him.

I know, Josh said, sucking on a sweetheart candy, his face a mass of caramel freckles, let's play Truth or Dare.

Truth, Sheryl said.

Okay, have you ever kissed Pete?

Sheryl turned the colour of red licorice and leaned forwards: Ask me something that isn't stupid, stupid.

Okay, do you have a crush on him?

I'm not playing, she huffed and crossed her arms not looking at either of them.

Does she or doesn't she? Only her hairdresser knows for sure, Josh snickered. Your turn, Pete.

Dare.

Okay, I dare you to eat ten sweetheart candies and smoke a cigarette at the same time. Peter obliged and they laughed at his chipmunk cheeks, the smoke escaping from his nostrils like a dragon while Josh directed, No, don't stop, you have to make smoke rings, that is soooo cool.

Okay your turn, Sheryl said.

Dare, Josh grinned.

Sheryl lifted her binoculars to her eyes and stared at him through them. Elementary my dear Watson, she said, seeing as Nancy Drew didn't have any cool expressions.

Okay climb on that garbage pail there, she told him, and say, I'm the king of the castle, loud.

You *are* a dirty rascal, Josh whined but he climbed up on the wire mesh pail all the same, hamming it up, pudgy arms spread wide in triumph, until he fell in, and they had to haul him out, giggling, and pluck the candy wrappers off him before Mrs. Wong came out and gave them all heck.

They sat in silence sharing the Twizzlers, watching some children skipping rope in the empty schoolyard. They were about to leave when an old black man appeared down the road, hair grey and frizzled and wild, small body bent under layers of dusty clothes. Even though it was the height of summer he wore a sweater and boots and strangely, a woman's flowered housedress over his trousers, as though the Salvation Army had run out of men's clothes. He carried a picking basket under one arm, and seemed to lurch and weave as he walked, following some inner rhythm with peculiar starts and stops.

Quick, don't look, Josh said, which they all promptly did. Stay really still, here comes the mad man of Cedar Hollow. Sheryl's red-haired cousin sat back, neck stiff, eyes staring straight ahead.

Sheryl peeked slyly up from her brown paper bag and whispered, Oh no, it's Harry Madeline, he's talking to himself again.

He's crazy, Josh whispered, and sometimes he rhymes like he's casting a spell or voodoo or something. Andy Vanderboch says he offers kids candy and then asks them to take their pants down. I heard he skins house cats and eats them. Sheryl shivered at this last. Then she and Josh pressed their faces in close, singing softly: *Mad, mad, Madeline, gone ahead and lost your mind* ... then dissolved in hushed conspiratorial giggling.

Shshshshshshsh!!!

Harry stooped at the roadside to pick up a small stone, then halted for a moment to regard the children with fierce eyes burning with some inner fire, and the children quickly studied their laps, moving their hands self-consciously about in them.

What you lookin' at? Harry shouted and the children shrank back owl-eyed.

Don't think I don't know you, Harry scolded, scuttling toward them enraged. Don't think I don't see ... I know the secrets of the Dark One, I seen his revels and his fornication. You best prepare for the day of the Lord, cause the lamb is on the throne, and his day of judgment comin'. He wagged a furious finger in Sheryl's face, while she shriveled ghostly-white against Peter.

Abruptly Harry turned on Peter.

Who do you think *you* be staring at? he yelled, reaching for something in his basket and the children shrieked and ran then, running until they were on the outskirts of town and Harry was far behind and they let go a collective sigh of relief and burst out in nervous giggling, talking all at once.

Whew, can you believe that? Josh said. Oh Slim, you're in trouble now, I think Harry likes you.

Shut up, Sheryl said, biting her lip, her breath ragged. Harry gave Sheryl that creepy Sunday night feeling. She picked at the Band-Aids on her thumbs.

They wandered back down the road chattering like noisy starlings, telling the adventure over and over, the story growing more outrageous and fearsome with each repetition, the three of them singing the song together all the way home. *Mad, mad, Madeline, gone ahead and lost your mind, and whosoever he shall find ... better be kind to mad, mad, Madeline.* Addressing the fields and the asphalt and the orchards with their chorus, as the sun began its lazy decline, and the hills of the escarpment veered purple in the distance. Singing until they were hoarse and worn out and grew quiet again.

Hey, Sheryl, Josh called, on the way home, having run on ahead and stopped in the road, I've got a present for ya.

Do not, she said.

Do so, he pestered, you'll really like it, I promise, close your eyes and open your hand, and she said no and he insisted and this went on for some time until he begged, and she relented and he dropped something into her palm saying, Watch this, to Peter. When she opened her eyes a dead bee nestled in the pink creases of her palm and she screamed as though shot, shaking the creature from her, hands flying up to her hair as if swatting away a swarm.

I hate you, she screeched and took off like a bullet, leaping over a gully full of cattails and wild asparagus and crashing through the bush while Peter ran after her, calling, Wait up, Slim, hey wait up, he was only kidding.

Sheryl streaked through the open field, dodging small shrubs and crabgrass, heading toward the forest below the hillside, the wind whistling, the grass hissing against her legs, a strange buzzing in her ears, in her head a little voice: *You're bad and I'm telling.*

The naked girl runs panic struck and blind, small body shivering with bees. Terror making her heels sing, tall black trees on either side, exploding in white blooms, feathery as cotton candy.

Sheryl scuttled around a few trees and fell, panting and clutching her side, onto the forest floor with its blanket of cedar needles, pink and sweet-smelling, and lay scratching at her skin, her head throbbing, and only then did she see Peter collapse beside her and hear Josh's voice following them all the way into the forest, muffled but complaining still.

Hey, you guys, Hey, WAIT UP! SHERYL-ANNE, PETE, WHERE ARE YOU? THAT'S NO FAIR.

Sheryl giggled, and once she started she couldn't stop, the *sight* had come again, and it was so scary she couldn't stop laughing, laughing being almost like crying, and Peter giggled also, and they lay there together giggling and listening as Josh crashed around in the brush for a few minutes, then gave up in disgust and shuffled back to the road whimpering, the sound of his footfalls gradually disappearing.

Sheryl stared up at the blue vault of the sky, waiting for her breath to quiet, the forest world safe and still, secretive, Peter lying on his back beside her.

Why'd you take off like that? he asked her.

I don't know, she said, embarrassed. And after a moment, it seemed hard to remember why she had been so scared all of a sudden, why she had run at all, so she said, I don't like bees, and, didn't you ever take off on your kid brother? All the time, Peter laughed, he was always yelling, Hey, wait up! Course I miss the little bugger now, he said sadly. He was always scared of the dark.

Peter sat up then to rest his back against the bark of a tree, and a shaft of light fell through the cedar branches and bathed his hair in yellow. For a moment, Sheryl felt safe from the voices, the *sight*. They were alone in the forest, the smell of cedar and the day's warmth lingering on their skin. Sheryl always felt good when she was with him, he made her feel calm and safe and lucky, all at once.

Close your eyes, she said to him.

Why?

Just do it.

Peter gave her a suspicious look but then did as she asked. He let his head fall back onto the bark of the tree, and before she lost her nerve and he could open his eyes, her mouth was on his, taking in the cigarette and licorice taste of him, smelling his sweet-and-sour boy smell. But in a second she grew frightened and rolled off him, laughing, Last one home's a dirty rotten egg, she said and sprinted off through the trees.

When Sheryl got home, Josh was standing on the porch red-faced and sobbing, You left me, you left me, and Eleanor shouted at her, We could just as easily have sent you off to the Children's Aid, her eyes glassy and mascara-smeared from too many vodka tonics and rage. Then Fergus was there and Sheryl was walking down the lane with him, her head hanging, her uncle scowling and angry, telling her she had disappointed him, she was his princess, and here she'd gone and let him down. She was supposed to look out for Josh, he was younger and smaller and she had been selfish, she was such a dark horse, such a blackhearted girl like her mother. Sheryl hung her head in shame. He said, After all I brought Peter home for you, and her eyebrows lifted, but then they were at Earl's abattoir, walking across the kill floor with its stench of spilt blood, Fergus lifting a hand in hello as he passed Earl and Jimmy Garrick watching from the office. Fergus opened the door of the giant freezer where the huge bovine bodies were hung and told her to go inside and think about what she'd done wrong, and when she was ready to say she was sorry she could come out. Sheryl was ready to say she was sorry right then and there and squeaked, Please don't, but the big metal door closed behind her all the same. As the light went out the headless bodies flashed before her eyes.

Scared you, didn't I? Sheryl said, tossing Peter an apple, moon-shaped and yellow. An apple a day keeps the doctor away. She was sitting in the tree, wearing overalls and a polka-dot blouse, her hair uncombed and untethered cascading over her shoulders, naked feet swinging free just above where she had discovered him lying asleep, mouth agape, guitar case lying open.

Peter caught the apple and tucked in his shirt and told her, no, he just didn't expect to see anybody was all.

Lifting her binoculars she zoomed in on his blue-brown eyes and thought about kissing him the other day and remembered how he had kissed back. When they ran away she would get a job at Woolworth's, serve coffee at the little diner and get fifty percent off all household merchandise. They would grow their hair long and dance the cha-cha at Yorkville cafes.

Did you know that in the old days gypsy girls chose their boyfriends by throwing apples at them? Eammon told me that.

You're too old for your years, Peter said. I came out to practice my guitar, he pointed to the instrument, grave and important and somehow exotic looking, lying in the wild grass. He pulled out a butt he'd stolen and lit it, squinting up at her.

Sorry about yesterday, he said.

That's okay, she shrugged, I'm always getting into trouble.

He asked if she'd gotten the strap. I used to get the belt from my old man, but the freezer—shit, was it cold?

No, I don't remember, I don't know, sort of.

You don't remember? Holy mackerel. Still, it's usually boys that do the kissing, eh, Slim.

She hung her head.

He reminded her that he didn't want a girlfriend, he was planning to skedaddle soon as harvest was over. She bit her lip, feeling him slip away, they were going to run away together, go to Toronto and find her mother, he just didn't know it yet.

It's a Yellow Transparent, she added, a July apple, one of the first, I picked it for you.

You're just a girl, Sheryl, he persisted, you're too young to be kissing the hired help.

I thought you were a folk singer, she pouted.

Well, that's true, he said, smoking thoughtfully.

Somewhere a lawn mower joined in with a rhythmic see-saw sound. Sheryl jumped down from the tree and took a puff of the cigarette. I'm not that young, she said, there's only three years difference between us. There's ten years between Eleanor and Fergus, three years is nothing.

Peter flushed, insisting three years was a lot, but Sheryl wasn't listening. Instead she dropped the straps on her overalls and lifted up her blouse revealing to him two little white breasts the size of tulip bulbs, blooming into pink nipples, and she watched as he went pale. His breath caught in his throat, and he said she was as crazy as Josh said.

Pull your shirt down, he said looking around, voice cracking, somebody could come.

But desperation made her brave and reckless and so she told him, Nobody can see us from here, silly, it's too far away. Go ahead and look if you want. Boys like looking at girls, I know it.

No, I'm not looking, he said, but he did look, and she asked him if he'd ever seen any before, and he said he had but only in his pop's girly magazines. Sheryl said, well at least hers were the real thing and close up.

Even though her heart was knocking so loud she thought she could hear it, she pulled her shirt right off so that she was now naked from the waist up and said breathlessly: You can touch them if you want.

Sheryl, he groaned.

Go on, she said.

Peter bit his lip. I could get in trouble, he stammered, you could get me fired ... but his voice trailed off unconvincingly, his eyes never leaving her body and she sighed, impatiently.

She lay down coquettishly on the long grass closing her eyes, her dark hair windblown, arms thrown out dramatically, Ophelia abandoned to the river, overalls floating down about her thin waist. She could feel the wind on her nakedness and lay listening to her own fretful breathing, wondering where she got the nerve. She was a mystery to her own self. Things were always popping out of her mouth before she could think better of them, and then it was too late to turn around. His hands were clammy and cold and they nervously tip-toed up the smooth diving board of her torso. She could feel something quickening in her and was surprised by the strange squirmy chain reaction of it all.

He said he had never touched anything so soft, and his voice was gentle, awestruck. Then he gave her a squeeze, and she sat up annoyed and swatted him away saying, Okay, that's enough.

They traversed the cedar forest, afternoon sunlight falling in a white haze through the spaces between trees, mosquitoes swarming their eyes, their noses, their lips and they slapped at them bored and irritated. It was now around three, the wind had died and the air was still and heavy. Sheryl walked on ahead picking a trail through a smaller deciduous grouping of maples and beech, elm and hemlock; ferns in profusion along the forest floor, moss on the underbellies of rocks. Eventually the trees grew sparse, and they entered a clearing with an old maple and a huge pink and grey boulder on the edge of a promontory overlooking the valley and the MacRae farm. Sheryl waited for Peter to catch up, and he came and stood beside her taking in the view, muttering, Holy smokes, isn't that something.

Listen, Sheryl said, and under the whine of mosquitoes they heard it—the sound of water. It's whispering, she said.

Sheryl led him along a path that followed a stream. The path dropped down, and the water trickled over a shelf of layered rock and emptied into a shallow pool below, a waterfall magically appearing among the trees, totally hidden from above. Sheryl took Peter down to the pool, and they clambered in behind the curtain of cool spray, crouching in the damp mouth of the cave behind the waterfall, listening to the gentle hissing of the falling water.

This is the coolest place, Peter said. Sheryl cupped her hands to drink, and he imitated her. The water was tart and tasted of moss and peat and rock. They could see the stream snaking down the valley, becoming a small finger pointing into the trees.

This is a special place, Sheryl said. They say trees and stones and water have spirits in them and if you listen real quiet you can hear what they're saying.

What do you mean?

They're whispering about their earth memories, about the seasons, they're remembering the passing of the icebergs and the coming of the first people here and together their sounds are the hum of the universe, like that sound in your ears at night. It's the last sound you hear before you die.

No shit, he said.

My Uncle Fergus told me that stones may be still, but they are watching and recording everything and you should always be careful what you say around them because your words go into the cosmic mind, into the Now.

Peter was silent. A purple dragonfly hovered above the pool and then darted off.

They scrambled back up to the lookout. Beyond Sheryl's favourite maple tree sprouted a wooden lean-to that resembled a teepee hastily assembled. There was a place for a campfire nearby with a ring of stones, and the lean-to had a tarpaulin nailed to the front for a door.

Sheryl lifted her arms: This is the summer place, she said.

Peter looked around, impressed. Sunbeams shone through the trees and scattered light on the forest floor, the huge boulder had rose-coloured veins running through it and they could hear the little stream.

I found it one summer when my grandma and grandpa were alive, Sheryl said, and we used to come here on holidays. Nobody comes here but me.

Nobody?

No—you're the first. I'm bringing you here because you're my friend. Peter frowned and kicked at the ground.

She made him promise on pain of death never to tell anyone about her secret place, and Peter rolled his eyes and said, Cross my heart and hope to die.

She went over to the lean-to and threw back the tarpaulin. Inside there was a mouldy blanket and a pillow, some magazines, a tin-can ashtray and a small basket full of mewling kittens. She crawled inside and sat cross-legged on the blanket and Peter followed her. She scooped up a kitten and placed it gently in his lap. The small creature let out a scratchy sound like a broken needle on a record, and Peter petted its black fuzzy head while the kitten rooted around in his palm. Sheryl carefully cradled another kitten, while the mother, Elizabeth Taylor, elegant and inky black, lay curled in the basket watching them.

April gave me this cat, Sheryl said. She's always taking in strays. She has six cats already and Uncle Earl won't let her keep any more. Elizabeth showed up at the abattoir one day and April said I could have her. I brought Elizabeth up here to have her kittens. I bring her milk and food from the barn every other day, Sheryl said.

Peter looked up at the walls and gasped, Holy mackerel, Slim, what are all those pictures? They're everywhere.

Sheryl had glued cutouts from magazines to the ceiling and walls. All of them dark-haired women. Mostly mothers with children, modeling coats or lingerie or little pillbox hats, selling ham or cigarettes, refrigerators or feminine napkins. Whether they were auburn, brunette or had hair black as shoe polish, they were all dark-maned and the children with them, little girls whose curls and outfits inevitably matched those of their sinewy photogenic mothers.

Holy smokes, Slim, Peter said, what have you done here?

That's my mother, Sheryl said.

But there's hundreds of them—how do you know which one is yours?

One of them is my mother. My Uncle Fergus says she's a fashion model. So I put lots up there, that way I know I won't miss her by accident.

Peter shook his head. You sure are something.

I dream about my mother sometimes, Sheryl said, leaning against the plank wall, her hair the colour of the midnight-haired cut-outs. In my dream she bends down to tuck me in and she smells like talcum powder and tobacco but I can't touch her and then she disappears.

Peter's birthday fell on a Saturday in July. The day the newspapers were splattered with pictures of the Harlem race riots, people smashing windows and throwing Molotov cocktails, black faces running from white faces, protesting the white shooting of a Negro boy. Still, all was peaceful in Eden Valley.

Standing in the kitchen, hands in his pockets, shrugging bashfully, not looking a day over sixteen, Peter announced to everyone he was turning nineteen and Sheryl didn't utter a word to the contrary. Fergus gave Peter a brand new Yamaha guitar, saying: I thought you might need something a little better to practice on, it's not a Martin or a Fender Telecaster I know, but the man at the store told me a Yamaha is a good learning guitar. It has six strings, chrome tuning heads and these nice white inlay thingamejiggies along the neck. I felt a young man with your talent, kiddo, should have himself a real guitar. Are you pleased?

Peter was so happy he kissed the guitar and shook hands with Fergus and played "Happy Birthday" for them all right there in the kitchen. Sheryl thought the new guitar was truly beautiful, blond like Peter himself. Eleanor baked Peter a cake, a large pound cake with a meringue guitar on top, and there were nineteen candles, Josh counted them.

After dinner, the usual pack came over to sit on the porch and drink Red Cap beer—the MacRae brothers, Fergus and Earl and Eammon and their wives, including April, who Josh and Sheryl secretly called Olive Oil and who smoked like a chimney, and Jimmy Garrick, Earl's fidgety partner at the abattoir, joined them later.

Sheryl parked herself by the hi-fi and played disc jockey, setting the controls for continual play and loading up the turntable with the latest albums: Bob Dylan, the Beatles, The Supremes, Petula Clark, Nat King Cole, Peter, Paul and Mary and the Four Tops. All the while, watching the men idly from the doorway.

Peter was radiant, he had slicked back his hair with Brylcreem like Fergus and it was shiny and coppery as new plumbing. He strummed his guitar Jezebel, *A guitar's got to have a name,* a cigarette tucked into a fret, the smoke curling up and puddling around his face.

They were discussing the coming harvest, and inevitably the conversation rolled around to the labour shortage. Many of the field crop farmers who usually came to pick would be busy this year, kids grew up and got on the bus to go into the big city now and never came back.

Fergus declared the answer was in mechanization.

Amen to that, the men said, giving Fergus their rapt attention, waiting for him to suggest a solution the way they did nowadays and Sheryl leaned her forehead against the screen door and wondered again how her uncle always knew just what to say or do next.

Carpe diem, Fergus said, seize the day. We're going to have to buy bulk bins, like they have in the neighbouring county and a brand new forklift. In the Orwellian future, Fergus predicted, everything will be done by machine.

The brothers grumbled about where the money could be had for such things, but he told them he would take care of it, and the mood shifted.

What's Or Well Yan? Josh asked, slipping in beside Sheryl where she crouched by the screen door.

It's another name for the new world, she told him.

That night they had a bonfire, and the men dragged the spring's dried apple prunings with their auburn-coloured branches into a clearing at the edge of the orchard and built a huge pyre. The firelight coloured their faces orange and the wood crackled, sending sparks like fireflies up into the starry night. Earl opened up a bottle of his infamous dandelion wine and poured everyone a cup. When the night grew cool, Sheryl wrapped herself in an old quilt beside Josh, staring, mesmerized by the fire.

Peter broke into a few bars of "On Top of Old Smokey," and when it came time for the chorus everyone sang along, shaking tambourines and rattles and clapping loudly when it was over, plying Peter with beer and cigarettes, shouting, Good show! Good show! Give us another one, maestro! Their voices trailing off into the night and echoing in the yard.

Gradually, the shadows in the orchard lengthened, the leaves whispering in the night breeze. Between the light of the fire and the darkness beyond there seemed a line, dividing the seen from the unseen, the said from the unsaid, day from night, separating the earthly plane from that other world where the unbelievable became real.

Suddenly Sheryl was aware of barking off in the distance. It was Lupus, his raspy protests riding the night wind, and she turned to Josh nuzzling in his sleeping bag beside her.

Josh, do you hear that?

Hear what?

Lupus?

He's barking, Josh said sleepily.

I know, he's been barking all this time, she said, ever since we came out here. He barks day and night in our yard, and yet I hardly ever *hear* him.

The thought that a thing could happen right in front of her, without her noticing, or hearing, or remarking on it at all, unsettled Sheryl. She peeled back the Band-Aid and worried her thumb again until it started bleeding. Soon Josh was snoring in a fleshy bundle beside her, wrapped in his flannel sleeping bag, a pudgy cheek smeared onto a squat hand. For a chilling moment she saw in his round face, a disappointed, bald and bitter old man.

They had worked through all the campfire songs they knew, 'She'll Be Comin' Round the Mountain," and the gospel tunes, "Swing Low, Sweet Chariot" among them and everyone was quiet now. A reefer went round the circle, and Peter put down Jezebel to accept the joint.

You're in Avalon, my boy, Fergus said mysteriously. Do you know what that is?

Sheryl watched as Peter shook his woozy head. She wished Fergus would pay as much attention to her as he did to Peter. Sometimes it seemed like her uncle could concentrate on only one person at a time.

Fergus adjusted his black-rimmed glasses and stared into the flames as though moved to speak by them. Avalon, the Isle of Apples. The ancients believed it was where Arthur went to die, and that's where we are, kiddo. In Eden. look at the apple trees all around.

Avalon, Peter whispered and sucked back the reefer. Cool.

Fergus lifted a long finger towards the sky with its stars big and small, and he pointed out the constellations: the Big Dipper, Little Dipper and Orion and the Bear, he knew them all. Then he pointed out a grouping of smaller stars with one bright star at the end, Polaris. Everyone was listening now, Eammon and Eleanor and April and Earl and Jimmy Garrick even. Fergus leaned his pointed intense face towards the boy and said: That is the circumpolar constellation *Ursa Minor*, or Little Bear, his tail is more commonly known as the Little Dipper. The ancient Greek sect known as the Cynics thought these stars looked like a dog. There's a famous prophecy about that one that not many people know. See how the north-pole star is the dog's tail?

They all followed Fergus's finger and Peter nodded.

Well, the Cynics believed that when the dog's tail moves from the north pole, the end of the world is at hand, and the universe will be plunged into chaos. You see, the loyal dog holds us in place.

Peter sat back and regarded the night sky with awe, his arms resting on the curved body of his guitar. Crazy, man, Peter said and took another toke.

Sheryl heard Lupus bark once, twice.

Let me tell you something else, Fergus said. They're different, the worlds of day and night. Never confuse them. One is ruled by the moon and the underworld, and the other by sunlight and earthly matters. What is right during the day is not at night and vice versa. If you live your life accordingly, it will be a rich and rewarding experience. Always remember that and you will know a higher truth, a greater liberation than most men know. *Sapere aude.* Dare to be wise.

Sheryl stretched out in her rocking horse pyjamas on the cushions by the open window, her transistor flattening her ear, filling her head with her favourite things. In her make-believe she was a maiden in Avalon, lying hair askew in the grass. Peter bent over to give her a kiss and she replayed this squirmy sexy part over and over again, drunk on the remembered cigarette, Juicy Fruit smell of him. Then they walked to her mother's house holding hands.

Suddenly she was interrupted by the sound of beer bottles toppling, the discordant thong of the guitar as it fell over and all the chords resounded at once. The adults were still partying out on the porch. Lupus barked a few times just to let the world know who was boss, and Sheryl looked out her window to see him standing, sniffing the air, luminous and white, an enchanted ghost-dog.

Dr. Beat said: *He-ey this is A L L Beat, that's Dr. Beat, keepin that sandman at bay. It's still summer and the weatherman says we've got more hot sunny days to come. So here's Martha and the Vandellas with "Heat Wave."*

Sheryl heard a noise on the stairs and turned to see Josh slouching in the doorway rubbing his eyes, wearing only his pyjama top and underwear. She loved him like a brother, but sometimes he could be such a pest.

Can I sleep in here with you?

Did you wet your bed again? she asked him. He hung his head and nodded. She felt sorry for him and relented. All right, but you have to sleep here by the window and if you wet my pillows I'll brain you.

Okay, he said, brightening and trotted over.

Pete's boss, isn't he? Josh said, climbing onto the cushions beside her.

Yeah, Sheryl sighed.

Who is Nancy Drew? he asked sleepily.

She's a girl detective. Her mom is dead and her dad's a lawyer and sometimes she helps him solve cases by snooping around, looking for clues, like Sherlock Holmes.

Oh, he said, is that who you want to be when you grow up?

Yeah, Sheryl said, I'm going to be a private detective.

Cool, Josh said. I want to be an astronaut.

He rested his cheek on a pudgy hand. Andy Vanderboch's brother Jeff told me that the last time anyone saw Ralph McDonald he was sitting on Harry Madeline's front step. There's a picture of Ralph in the police station. Mrs. McDonald doesn't think he ran away, she swears somebody kidnapped him. They lay there for a moment listening to the wind skipping through the orchard.

You ever notice how nighttime smells like gingerale? Josh asked.

Late that Sunday night they drove in the Bonneville, moths fluttering under the oval eyes of lamps strung out along the highway as the car swooned by, entering Cedar Hollow and humming through the quiet town, until they slipped out the other side and plunged into the all-encompassing darkness.

Fergus and Peter sat in the front seat smoking Rothmans, chatting in the blue light of the car's instrument panel, while Josh slept in the back on top of some sleeping bags, and Sheryl lay beside him, clutching a pillow, pretending to be asleep, watching summer swoop by outside the car windows. Earl and Eammon followed in Earl's Buick, Eleanor and April in the back seat. Sheryl could occasionally see the lights of the Buick, appearing on a hill behind them, then momentarily lost in a valley only to reappear again seconds later.

They stopped at a road sign to turn a corner, and Sheryl sat up to stretch. There in the ditch lay the rigid body of an animal, unfortunate road kill. For a moment she thought it was a horse, with its long legs at odd angles, equine eyes staring into an uncaring sky, dried blood in dark spittle at its muzzle. Looking at it Sheryl felt the breath rush out of her. In a moment, she saw it was a deer and realized her mind was playing tricks on her and she pulled a blanket around her thin shoulders.

Where are we going?

Go back to sleep, her uncle said.

I keep hearing meowing, like there's a kitten somewhere in the car, Sheryl said.

It's all in your mind, Slim, lie down, Fergus said. Sheryl has an overactive imagination, he whispered to Peter.

Sheryl had been awakened by Eleanor in the dead of night. Eleanor told her to get dressed, explaining they were going camping, and Sheryl had shuffled out to the waiting car, wondering why they had to go at two a.m. Fergus was prone to these crazy whims as if some light bulb snapped on in his head, and it didn't matter what time of day or night, he would say, There's no time like the present, kiddo, and hustle them out of doors.

I can't get back to sleep, Sheryl sulked now, and her uncle handed her his flask. I don't know why we couldn't go camping tomorrow, she whined, but he gave her a look in the rear-view mirror that made goosebumps pop out all over her arms and she was quiet. She took a swig from his flask, but the liquid tasted bitter and made her cough, so she gave it back and lay her head against the window, still wide awake, grateful for the cool, damp night air, listening to the conversation in the front seat of the car.

Fergus was talking, his voice like a dull siren in the darkness, intense, rushing. He had this fast start-and-stop way of talking sometimes, he was staring at the road, glancing over occasionally towards Peter, and Sheryl could see his eyes were big and black behind his boxy glasses, his face blue-lit and wild.

I'm taking you to a special place, kiddo, he said to Peter, a sacred place, ritual place of the ancients, my boy. It's a secret very few people round here know about, and it's in the park where we'll camp overnight. You can't go there just any time. Tonight's the night to be there, he said and gripped the steering wheel as if urging the car on.

People around here believe it's an Indian burial site, but I know a fella from Warmwater believes it was built by the Celts, hundreds of years ago.

Fergus adjusted his glasses and rubbed his temple with one large hand.

Not too many people will tell you this, kiddo, and they don't write about it in books. Archeologists say the Celts didn't get to the new world until Columbus, but there's an old tale about a Father Brendan who made the journey in a leather boat hundreds of years ago. There's those that think other red-bearded men like himself made the trip and started a trading empire, sailing up and down the Great Lakes collecting copper from the Indians to take back home.

Cool, Peter said.

It's a temple to the natural world. In the old days they had a doorway so that you could enter inside, and there were gatherings there by torch light and rocks on top placed just so that told the time and the seasons. You have left the old world behind, Fergus chuckled. You have been sent to us. Chosen.

Peter giggled as if there were some private joke between them, and there was the sound of a struck match, and the car had that funny reefer smell, a cross between incense and a burning lawn. Sheryl couldn't help shivering.

The headlights of other cars approached and swooped across the roof of the Bonneville, then faded and were no more, and Sheryl watched their passing feeling hollow and shriveled. She could see the moon outside, a ring around its full white face making it look possessed, bathing the night world an eerie blue. Peter's window was open, and his hair was mussed by wind, and he looked roguish, unkempt, like a drifter from the trailer park outside of town.

Of course, Fergus said after awhile, you can't possibly go without the magic pill, and he handed the boy a Pez container and they both ate the candies, sniggering in the dark.

Soon Fergus had launched into his million questions. Tell me son, what do you want from life? What's your *modus operandi*, your goal? Peter shrugged bashfully and said maybe he'd like to cut an album one day or shucks, go on tour. He thought it would be cool to travel around in a Volkswagen bus with his girlfriend, play in coffee houses.

Fabulous! Fergus said smacking the steering wheel. Don't be afraid to dream.

Sheryl fancied herself the girl in the bus. She would wear paisley with striped stockings and maybe learn to play a tambourine.

Peter seemed to gain confidence as Fergus urged him on. His record, if he ever made one, he said, would have his name on the front, *Peter Angelo*, just him sitting there with Jezebel on his knee. Maybe smoking and not laughing or smiling, looking serious like a folk singer ought to. And when he'd made some money Peter was going to bronze the blond Yamaha Fergus had given him and buy himself a brand new guitar, a Gibson Hummingbird guitar. That was his dream, by gosh. He had wanted to be a singer ever since he was eight years old and saw Johnny Cash on television.

Fabulous! Fergus said again, stick with me, kiddo. We can make it happen.

It grew quiet now in the cab as they stared ahead at the road, smoke obscuring their faces, cricket song floating in from the open windows, while privately Sheryl fretted, afraid they would both run off without her. Everyone was always leaving her behind. First her mother, then her grandparents. Besides, it gave her the creeps when Fergus and Peter smoked up and started making crazy plans.

I always feel like I can talk about stuff to you, Peter confessed. You never laugh at me, like my old man would have done.

Think of me as your friend, your teacher, Fergus nodded. I can see it all now—*Peter Angelo's Greatest Hits!*

Peter laughed and checked himself out in the side mirror. Sheryl had never known a boy to look at himself so much. But then maybe that was just the way pretty people were.

Remember to think big, Fergus said. It is only necessary to inflame the will with the proper passion. Once you've got a few songs together, I have friends in Toronto you could stay with while you check out Yorkville. In the meantime, there are tricks I can teach you, short cuts, ways to make things go your way. Devices for bending the laws of the universe, let's say...

Sheryl's bedtime orange drink finally took its effect and she succumbed to the rocking of the car on the road, sleeping fitfully off and on in the cramped cocoon of the back seat. When she awakened later the car was full of smoke, and they were talking about philosophy, about living in the Now, about a man named Timothy Leary, their voices quick and urgent.

Leery, leery, Sheryl thought saying the word over and over in her sleepy mind, thinking of eyeballs for some reason, a tall skinny man maybe with big bloodshot eyeballs. Outside the valley was bathed in mist, and they hurtled blind through the darkness, the world shadowy, unreal.

The car lurched and corrected itself.

Sheryl heard the kitty meowing again, and that distracted her from their conversation. She felt sure she wasn't imagining it, the sound was coming from the trunk, and she wondered what a kitten would be doing back there. Everything was all mixed up in her mind, the cigarette smoke, the kitty, *meow*, the men talking, the outlines of things frantic with static like snow on the television and she succumbed once more to sleep and the car's gentle rocking....

The girl dreams that she is sleeping and awakens in the black-and-white world. She is alone in a car and the door has been left open. The overhead bulb throbs dully and moths flutter around the light. She doesn't know where she is. Worse, she doesn't know who she is. She stumbles on out into the night, lost and alone. There is a path.

She glimpses firelight through leaves, follows the smell of burning wood. Walking, her toes barely touching ground, lured on by the sound of music and far-off laughter.

Above, the moon is a white face through a window. The ground is moist, and the air hums with the sound of frogs and tree toads.

She steps into a clearing. There are men and women half-naked. They hold a boy down and a kitten aloft. Someone takes a knife and draws the blade across the kitten's neck. Its screaming is silenced although the little teeth still open and close, helpless. There is blood everywhere, splashing red, all over the face of the boy, on the hands and arms of the others. They mark their bodies with the blood in slashes like war paint.

The girl turns and thumps back down the forest path, her feet hitting down, down. She can hear her heart beating, the sound loud and hollow inside her head like a church organ, the music rising into the vaulted ceiling and scattering startled birds.

In the morning, Sheryl stumbled outside into the dawn air, robins chirping, a truck passing somewhere far off on a highway with a lonely hypnotic sound that kept time with the throbbing in her temples. She remembered herself somewhere in a gully after tripping and falling face down into pine needles and knew only then that she was awake and walking. Before her was a moss-covered rock, cool and green, and she collapsed there momentarily, fingered its damp spongy body and realized only that she did not know where she was, or where she had been for some time now, or why she tottered clutching a sleeping bag, bleary-eyed and lost, along an unfamiliar forest path.

It had happened again. Time had slipped away from her, it had a way of doing that, a thing shameful and frightening that she kept to herself, convinced this aberration was the result of some awful fault in her, and the slip made her question everything, including who she was.

She dusted herself off and continued on quietly, the forest massive and expanding before her eyes. The leafy canopy was alive with raucous and frightful sounds: a whippoorwill shrieking from a treetop, the morbid hum of mosquitoes, a chipmunk scurrying in the underbrush. She rushed forward, panicked, starting at every little disturbance, until mercifully she burst through an opening in the trees and found herself by a small campfire, and was amazed to see the others, milling about nonchalant and unwashed, as though she'd never been missed. She recognized the place then by the sacred mound rising up in a small clearing behind them.

She was so relieved she sank to her knees. The campsite had stones in a circle, burnt logs in the centre, and there was one large boulder on top of the Sacred Mound, looking ominous on the plateau above. Sheryl scratched at a ring of mosquito bites, the sight of the place sending waves of foreboding through her.

She got up and trotted over to the small circle where her odd family sat silently eating breakfast cereal in tin bowls and drinking coffee, oblivious that she had been lost. Eleanor, her hair parted in the middle and ironed straight like a peroxided peacenik, wore moon-shaped beads and a rumpled peasant smock, and April sat beside her in a sleeveless shift, the men in jeans. Peter wore his red kerchief Aunt Jemima-style around his head, and Fergus looked dramatic as ever in large black riding boots and the poofy white shirt of a troubadour. He was washing his hands with a small bottle of alcohol he kept in the glove compartment of the car. He produced a nail file and filed an edge clean.

Sheryl felt bedraggled and filthy. She looked over at Peter. His eyes were swollen, and there were lines on his cheek from sleep. She waved, but he ignored her, walking over to chat with her uncle. She hated the way he shadowed Fergus everywhere these days, as if he no longer had a mind of his own. Everyone loved Fergus and tried to please him. She wished Peter felt that way about her. Nothing was fair in this world.

Helping herself to an orange, she poked at the cold fire with a sneakered toe, asking no one in particular, Who did this?

Eleanor answered without looking up from her cereal. Maybe the faeries have been here.

Why didn't we see them then? asked Josh, emerging from his sleeping bag by the fire.

Because they're invisible, Fergus said. This rang true to Sheryl, she frequently felt invisible, invisible as air or wind, empty and shallow, a ghost of a girl no one noticed.

Why? she asked. Why are they invisible?

Because they're beautiful and naked, Eleanor said, and they don't want people to see them.

The others laughed, enjoying some private joke.

They live in the forest at night and only come out on the full moon, Fergus said. A long time ago you could see them everywhere, but they were hunted, persecuted, and now for hundreds of years they've been in hiding.

Why? Sheryl asked again, feeling cranky.

Fergus turned away to tell the women they should start packing up. Silently Earl's skinny wife April rose and began to put things away. Sheryl noticed that April's hands were shaking.

Do they give you nightmares? Josh asked, looking bewildered, scratching his carrot-coloured brush cut. 'Cause last night I had nightmares.

But no one answered him. Sheryl tossed her orange peel into the cold fire and wiped her sticky hands. She thought he was lucky, she had had nightmares ever since she could remember.

Sheryl sat in the front seat of the pickup with Eammon, face out the window, feeling the wind, the wheat and corn on either side of the road high and shushing and whirling occasionally like a crazed dervish. She hung out the window to wave at Peter in back, huddling under a tarpaulin looking self-sorry and miserable. But he wouldn't catch her eye, he was avoiding her but she didn't know why. Some of the earlier varieties of apples were ready, the Yellow Transparents and Red Askertons, and with orchard work picking up it seemed like there was never any time for fun these days. His skin was tanned dark from the sun, his hair lemon-coloured, his fingernails dirty and his face tired.

The sky had put a swift end to orchard work; it was okay to work through rain, but lightning was out of the question, so Eammon decided they should go into town this afternoon to the hardware store to pick up odds and ends, and Sheryl had begged to go. Uncle Eammon had agreed but insisted Peter sit in the back of the truck. She had wanted to ride in the back too, saying she didn't care if she got wet, she wasn't afraid of a little rain anyhow, but Eammon said she was a young lady now, and she should get into the cab and hush up.

She sat in the front seat scowling beside him, sorry she'd ever asked, cursing the meanness in him, that little voice inside her head saying over and over, *I hate you, I hate you*, until she calmed down.

Then the sky broke. The rain fell in tunnels until everything was waterlogged. Sheryl sat staring through the swipe of the windshield wipers, still pouting, listening to their *swish, swash, swish, swash*, her clothes and skin all sticky, the air in the cab growing damp and close with the windows rolled up. Eammon had the radio on, but he never listened to anything modern, having developed a taste for classical music from his days as a trucker when Grandpa MacRae was alive and ran the farm with Earl. He was tuned to a station that played opera, and a bold soprano wailed into the tiny cab, making the ride that much more unsettling and theatrical.

You have a schoolgirl crush on that boy, don't you? he said suddenly, breaking the silence.

No, Sheryl lied, blushing, the music swelling into a crescendo while the sky was stung by lightning.

Well, you know nothing good will come of it.

So? Sheryl sulked.

You know what happens, Slim, he continued, almost sadly. This isn't a story that can have a happy ending now is it? he asked. And he smiled at her then, as though trying to be helpful, but the gap in his teeth was a yawning pit that made him look like a jack o' lantern, ghoulish and menacing, and she turned away from him.

I don't know what you're talking about, Sheryl said primly, shaking her untidy pigtails, jiggling her knees together, her heart stuttering in recognition of some truth in what he said. He laughed again, a cracked dry laugh that split itself open with a strange bitterness.

Don't you now, he said, well, then Slim, you don't know yourself.

She felt shivers up and down her skin, and he turned the music up louder, smoldering beside her, some mysterious fury burning in him that frightened her. His anger seemed to be one with the crackle of lightning, and she was afraid, worried that he might do something rash, something dangerous, that he was capable of something awful.

But the lightning wore itself out, and in minutes the rain had stopped. The opera seemed to soothe him also, and they rolled down their windows to discover the world brightly green again from the rain wash, clean as a new-painted house, robins hopping on lawns and sparrows splashing in puddles.

He lit up a cigarette that he had hand-rolled from a small pouch of sweet-smelling tobacco that he kept in his pocket. Sheryl saw Levon up on the gravel shoulder ahead, walking with a decrepit dog, and she leant out her window and waved at him and he stopped, his face wan and unsmiling, lifting a palm.

Eammon offered her some of his cigarette but she said, no thank you, with exaggerated politeness, and he scoffed: You mean to tell me you don't smoke? She shrugged and said sometimes she just didn't feel like it. He said nothing concentrating on the road, driving on until they got into town, and he pulled up in front of Hillman's Hardware.

Peter emerged from under the tarpaulin bedraggled and irritable, and Eammon clapped him on the back, laughing, and said he was one tough son of a gun. He gave Sheryl money for them both to go get an ice cream in the park while he took care of business inside.

They wandered over to the little parkette by the water where there was an ice-cream truck, music tinkling while it sat parked by the curb. Sheryl chose strawberry and Peter had chocolate, and they ate their cones standing up, because the bench had a puddle in it from the recent downpour, facing the giant apple opposite. It was a huge round wooden apple, large as a small cottage and painted cherry red, which acted as the tourist information booth and looked silly having been dropped smack dab in the middle of the sidewalk.

Isn't that the funniest thing you ever saw? Peter said, and Sheryl nodded.

It's been there two years now, for people coming up in summer to the beaches in apple country.

They licked their cones and watched the apple. A head appeared in the booth suddenly, popping up from below, and Sheryl saw that it was Marianne Vanderboch from next door, her perky face a vision of adolescent perfection, shiny blond hair in a pony tale, perfect smile. She wore a crisp white blouse and a little red hat the colour of the apple that framed her.

She waved, and they waved back, and Peter muttered quietly, as if talking to himself, She sure is pretty, eh?

Sheryl felt her heart sink, his words like a slap, suddenly she hated strawberry and said so then sat stunned, speechless, feeling like an awkward child wearing pigtails and dirty seersucker shorts, old beaten-up Keds.

As if he sensed the wound his words had caused her, Peter added, Of course you're a pretty girl too, Slim, you just don't take care of yourself.

To make matters worse, the ice cream toppled out of her hand and onto her leg, and they were forced to busy themselves wiping the mess off her skinny thigh, while her mortification deepened and she despaired of ever having a boyfriend.

Meanwhile, Peter prattled on about how Fergus wanted to take his picture for his resume. Sheryl's uncle knew an agent in Toronto who could hook him up with the right people, get him gigs playing in all the folk clubs: the Purple Onion and the Bohemian Embassy and the Village Corner Club. Fergus and Peter were going to make the trip together, paint the town.

The ice-cream truck drove off playing, "Three Blind Mice" with a high-pitched tinkling that set Sheryl on edge. She felt misery open its jaws and swallow her whole.

If Bob Dylan could be a nobody one day and a star the next, Peter rattled on, maybe I could too. Fergus told me I'm a better singer than Dylan, way better than a lot of them. Fergus is the best, Peter said, he told me I am going places, man.

Sheryl padded past the living room on her way upstairs when she heard her uncle call out her name. He was sitting in the dark wearing his smoking jacket, a satin waistcoat that reminded her of gentlemen with English accents in Saturday afternoon matinees. Fergus always did like dressing up. He was smoking, legs crossed in the eggplant-coloured chair, reading by the light of one small lamp, underlining a paragraph in a dusty hardcover. He was often bent over some book and she was curious about what he was writing, underlining, thinking inside his mysterious severely combed head.

He looked up at her. Sit down, sit down it's time we had a little chat.

She perched on the corner of the chesterfield, and he asked her what she wanted most in life? She shrugged, confused by the enormity of the question and nervous, sensing a test. She admitted that she wanted to be a private investigator, wincing as she heard her own words, knowing that this sounded grand and ridiculous compared to nursing and teaching and airline stewardessing, which were the ambitions of most young girls her age.

So then you want to snoop in other people's lives? he asked, disdainfully.

Well, no not really, if you put it like that...

Then what do you want now before you grow up and become a detective?

I don't know.

I'm sure you must, he glared at her, and again she had the eerie feeling he could read her thoughts, and she mustn't lie.

I guess I want, well I would like to be Peter's friend, she confessed.

His friend, ahhh. He seemed pleased by this answer.

I want to be his friend, yes, she shrugged again, casting her eyes at the hardwood floor, regretting every word. She could see only half of Fergus's face in the darkness, but she knew he was in one of his moods. Her uncle was prone to these bouts of questions, she and Josh called it Truth and Lies.

What are you after, Slim? he demanded after a minute and she blanched.

I guess, I guess I want him to like me, she whispered, biting her lip.

I see, and what are you doing so that he will?

She was surprised by this. I don't know, I'm friendly?

Friendly, hmmm, he said in an even voice. If you want him to like you and be happy here you must ask yourself are you making him feel at home? Like one of the family? Peter is your charge, kiddo. You're to see that he becomes an asset to us because whatever happens to him it's your responsibility.

Yes, sir, she returned. Can I go now?

No, he said matter-of-factly, but she burst into tears then, spluttering that she wished Fergus would stop filling his head with hare-brained ideas. Everybody was always leaving her, and with that she dashed up the stairs two at a time to her room, slamming the door.

She crouched inside her closet, among the scattered shoes and empty suitcases and cried until, as Eleanor would say, she got it all out of her system, then she tried on all her clothes, throwing half of them out.

They were necking in the teepee, lying on an old mouldy blanket, the kittens mewling and nursing around them, a hundred dark-haired Cleopatras looking down from above. Sheryl was teaching Peter French kissing and she held him close, smelling the orchard in his hair, feeling the heat rise in him, life sun-kissed and delicious with potential when he was near.

I hope you know that we're just friends, he said peevishly, breaking away, I could get in trouble for this. Besides I can't kiss with all those pictures looking down on me. It's like a million people watching us. And now you've gone and given me a boner, I won't be able to sit down for a week. Don't go getting ideas in your head.

I never did, Sheryl said, desultory, wiping her mouth with the back of her hand, picking at her white shoelace. She had put on clean shorts this morning and had even tamed her unruly hair. She checked now to see that the little pony barrette was still in its place, then she gave him the two dollars they'd agreed on so he could buy cigarettes.

Thanks, he said sulkily. I just didn't want to take any money out of the bank account Fergus has for me. He's saving money for my trip to Toronto in the winter. I'm getting $1.25 an hour. It adds up. He got me a bank book and everything. Want to see it? I'm collecting interest.

No, Sheryl said, what's fair is fair.

Peter lit up a cigarette and leaned his blond head against the plank wall. How come you know so much about kissing?

Sheryl wasn't sure, she felt a momentary flutter of fear. She sat up and pulled a butt out of her blouse pocket, lit it with her cowboy lighter and regarded him. I don't know, I don't remember. Why do I always have to explain everything? You're as bad as Josh.

He looked back at her with heavy-lidded eyes, his face pinched and cranky as a tired baby's. I miss my dog, Buddy, he would like it here,

Peter said. I'm beat. This apple picking is killing me, man, it's no good for an artist.

It's smoking dope and drinking that's killing you, she said petulantly. That stuff will stunt your growth.

Peter laughed and told her she was a goody two-shoes. Your uncle says the rules in the world were made to be broken.

You don't have to do everything Fergus says, she pouted. It was always Fergus this and Fergus that these days, and she was sick of it. Still, she didn't push the issue, no one ever criticized Fergus.

She examined her bronco lighter where the brown horse was bucking its red rider, who held on valiantly in the midst of a creamy-coloured plastic world. She twirled the lighter around in her hand, threw it in the air, caught it, snapped the top back and flicked the starter into dazzling flame in one smooth move, just like a cowgirl.

Heigh-ho, Silver! she called out, imagining herself Dale Evans but Peter ignored her. Sheryl squashed the cigarette under her sneaker. You have bad breath anyway, she said. She stuck her long lean legs, naked but for shorts and small white socks, out the tepee. She had on the same freshly ironed pink blouse that she'd worn to church this morning and was annoyed he hadn't noticed her recent efforts at personal grooming. There were clouds now, armies of cotton horses, cats and old ladies formed and reformed in the wind highway above. The kittens purred in their basket. She looked over at them, then looked closer.

Hey, one of the kittens has gone missing, she said, and it's my favourite one, the black one with white boots and a horse's name, National Velvet. Sheryl got up and rummaged around the teepee, checked outside too.

I can't find her, she said, when she got back. She picked up each one of the kittens in the basket and petted them with exaggerated tenderness.

Peter looked at her for a moment. Maybe it wandered off, he said.

Sheryl cradled a squirming tabby and sighed. Sometimes, she said, the bigger ones will eat the runt. Sometimes even mother cats eat their own babies. I don't know why they do that, she mused sadly. I wonder how long she's been gone. I'll have to bring them all down to the barn soon as fall comes. She put the tabby back carefully and stroked its fuzzy head.

Come on, she said, slipping out of the teepee into the air, and Peter came after her. She started walking along the ridge away from the farm, getting dangerously close to the edge, the binoculars swinging from side to side where they hung around her neck. She had a stick in one hand and was picking at the ground, poking at ostrich and walking ferns, lady slippers and hart's tongue, walking under maple, beech, ash and sycamore, when Peter caught up with her, brushing twigs and dust off his behind.

She told him that they were walking along the Niagara Escarpment, a thing created by God, it was so old. A huge glacier had come through here millions of years ago, before there were cattle or Indians and chiselled this hillside and left millions of fossils. They foraged for a moment, and Peter found a rock and cracked it open and they examined the fossil under the binoculars. A perfect little creature appeared, its spine and wings embedded in rock.

Sheryl took him to Petun Rock, a large grey-black rock jutting out of the forest into the sky in a peak. Moss clung to the rock's sides like a furry skin. Sheryl and Peter shouted into a cave and their voices leapt back at them. A cool draft emanated from the cavity like the air from a basement, only cleaner, chilled, primordial air, that no one else had muddied by breathing. They clambered up Petun Rock's ruddy sides, grasping at branches of stunted spruce until they got to the top and looked down on the little valley, the hillside like a postcard of a still and perfect summer day, the drop dizzying below.

Only six more weeks of summer, Sheryl sighed.

The wind picked up and sent her hair into her face, and she closed her eyes and stood still, feeling the wind tickle the backs of her knees, cool the insides of her elbows. Such a relief after the long heat wave. The rustling in the trees seemed to speak of something coming, some change. The wind always picks up in August, she told him, and felt sad for no reason she could name.

They climbed back down and walked on through the forest until they hit the road, and she took him to the pioneer cemetery, a small acre of green lawn shaded by a clutch of aspen, just off County Road Ten. They walked among the bleached graves, with their faded eulogies to *rest in peace* and *be forever blessed*. Sheryl wondered aloud: Will anyone remember us when we're dead and gone? She cocked her small face to look at him, but Peter just shrugged, lost in his own thoughts.

On the way back she told him about her recurring dream. In the dream she was on a hillside with teepees all along the slope, and as she descended she heard the sound of drumming and a man came out of a teepee, carrying a stick. When she looked more closely she saw that on the stick there was the bloody head of a horse, big teeth grimacing. The evil medicine man thumped the head up and down, up and down, like it had magical powers, and somehow she knew that he had been doing this for a long time, and she woke up terrified and sweating.

Peter shook his head and said, Holy smokes, Slim, it's a wonder you get any sleep at all.

It's always been like that, she said. It gets worse every summer I spend here. I wonder if I'll ever sleep like normal people. She paused, thinking there were other things she might tell him but decided not to.

I love horses, she mused out loud. They're my favourite animal. Did you know Northern Dancer was the first Canadian horse to win the Kentucky Derby? He won the Preakness and the Queen's Plate too before he injured his leg. Now they're not sure if he'll ever race again. She plucked a piece of prairie grass and twirled it between her fingers.

One night I dreamt of black water and the next morning my Nana died.

Cool, he said, then added, sorry.

She told Peter her grandpa had died of cancer and her grandma had fallen face forwards into her ice cream at the dinner table one year later.

Yeah, my grandparents are long gone too, Peter said. Granny Angelo reeked of garlic and Absorbine Junior. I could never understand a word she said. Sheryl laughed and said she was sorry too.

They went by the Crazy River, dotted with milkweed and Queen Anne's lace, and heading back home along a different route, they passed the sad dilapidated shack with uneven shingles where the Indians lived. It was surrounded by a natural border of poplars and birch, and they walked slowly by, sneaking shy looks at the Indians sitting around a small campfire smoking and drinking tea. There was an odd assortment of car parts and mattresses and broken children's toys in the yard. The Indians turned wary faces to watch the boy and girl pass.

Sheryl and Peter hurried back up the road until they got to the old-growth forest again, and Sheryl suddenly stopped and said they were the relatives of the Indians her Uncle Eammon was going to hire for the harvest. She had never seen where they lived up close before.

They stood for a moment looking out through the weather-bent cedars perched on the ridge, down into a small valley below, where the gnarled rooty world of the escarpment abruptly ended and a new world began, a man made world, full of fields and meadows and orchards. The ridge was a border they couldn't cross over.

The wind scurried around their feet, and Sheryl heard it whisper inside her head: *Don't go any further.* So she stood, looking through her binoculars, hand holding back her whirlwind hair, Peter peering over her shoulder. The little valley was surrounded on all sides by hills and forest and formed almost a perfect bowl, protected on all sides, hidden from the rest of the landscape, the town and the farms to the north, the shadow of the ancient ridge falling over it.

On the bottom there was a small meadow of scrub grass that had yellowed from the hot sun, and the parched earth shone through in places, sandpaper dry and cracking, little tufts of grass and weeds growing sparsely like old hair on a balding scalp.

Peter borrowed the binoculars and said, What's that? pointing to an old barn. Its blanched wooden sides still stood on stone foundations, while the roof was open to the heavens at one end, and the door lingered ajar on one of the hinges. The remains of another smaller stone building lay to the side like an older sibling, and as the wind blew the loose door swung wide with a creaking groan, and goosebumps leapt up Sheryl's thin arms. Even more odd, the open field was littered with abandoned appliances, an old stove and four refrigerators, arranged in a circular formation.

Wow, look at that, Peter said, marvelling at it all.

It's Sunday, Sheryl said, as though she'd just remembered. There had been church as usual in the morning, but afterwards Fergus had not felt up to the afternoon drive. She felt the Sunday-night feeling coming on.

Don't tell, the whispers said, and Sheryl went blank standing there in the cool shade of the forest, some numbness settling in her limbs, a small ache spreading between her ears.

Well, what is it? Peter said.

Kitchenhenge, Sheryl said.

What? Peter asked.

That's what Fergus calls it, Sheryl said. It's some garbage and a barn, what does it look like?

Well, I know but...

Don't tell.

It's the old barn, Sheryl said, scratching her skin, old mosquito bites suddenly itchy again. Fergus's great grandfather's. The one who came to Canada from the old country.

Cool, Pete said, let's go look. But Sheryl shook her head, no, complaining it was too warm out in the open sun. The boy walked the edge of the crest looking for a way down, strangely revitalized, determined to check it out.

He mustn't see.

Her body followed him, the whispers threatening, saying no, her legs doing whatever they pleased.

This way, she told him, surprised by her own voice, you can't get there from that side. She showed him another route down the overhang, a small path cutting through chickweed and dandelion, winding around the base of the cliff-face, behind Sheryl's summer place, and then there it was: Kitchenhenge.

Peter walked towards the buildings, approaching the dark skeletal barn, the stone foundations of the old house, the cracked stone floor growing St. John's Wort and burdock for carpet, comfrey by the front door. Peter entered the open doorway, and jumping from stone to stone, he called out cheerfully, Hey, this could have been the kitchen. The bathroom was probably over here.

He returned to the decaying barn with the hole in the roof. Let's go inside, he shouted to her.

Sheryl hesitated outside while he opened the barn door, and it swung wide, swallows startling up into the mouth of the open sky. Inside there was evidence of life, on one wall a giant painted eye, the size of a human head, stared out at them with a blue rim and red iris. To the left of the eye was written the numbers: 11:11. Peter turned to the door where Sheryl hovered, a small shadow in the frame.

Will you get a load of that? he said. Isn't that something else?

He strutted back and forth in front of the eye, declaring that wherever he walked it followed, always looking straight at him.

I wonder who did that? he mused out loud.

Sheryl had come in and stood just inside the door facing the giant eye. Below there was a large slab of stone, and Peter went up and ran his hand along the smooth marble, and she shivered as though he had touched her skin. She scratched her elbow, there was a buzzing in her ears, a cacophony of worry and warning growing inside her. On top of it all, she was getting a headache. The voice said: *Don't touch, don't go near.*

Who do you think did that? Peter repeated again.

Kids, Sheryl said. I don't know, I don't remember.

You don't remember? Peter said.

Sometimes I just don't remember things, she said, her head throbbing.

Looks as though people come here a lot.

Let's go, she said.

He stepped backwards and nearly tripped over the handle of a trap door.

Well, now look at that, he said and bent to open it.

Sheryl's foot came down. He would have to lift her weight too, if he wanted to go any further.

Let's go, she said, her voice cracked and thin. We have to go now she insisted, and her face was so strange and pale, he asked if she was sick or something.

Outside, he ran around the rusting appliances, opening doors, laughing, boldly defying her while she stood and watched him. The valley was full of moans, the barn and appliances a place of ghosts. There were flies whining in the grass at their feet. He came over to where she sat on a log and asked her what was wrong.

Bad things happen here, she said.

Baloney, he countered. Her head was cocked listening, the whole valley howling in her head. On the other side of the barn, there was an open barbecue pit and the remnants of a campfire. Peter walked over and stood nosing a burnt log with the toe of his shoe. The log lay in a halo of ash, charred and cold, the black cinders of its flesh cracked and wizened as an old face. Peter toyed with the old wood.

There's been a fire here not too long ago.

Crouching down on his haunches, he rubbed the ash through his fingertips like the fine sand of time, musing, Who do you figure comes to this place?

Sheryl tweaked a piece of wild carrot from the earth's parched floor and let the wind carry off the little feathery seeds.

This is a magic place, she said.

Magic? Peter snorted, his yellow head bleached and shiny in the late-day sun. That's just an old wives' tale, Sheryl-Anne.

My Uncle Fergus told me, she said, scratching a mosquito bite on her elbow and squinting in the sun to look at him. She had a bracelet of bites around her ankle, and they started to pester her now.

He's seen faeries here at night. They live under the escarpment and in the hills, near streams and graveyards, by the sacred mound. And they come out on the full moon and build fires and dance naked.

They stood there, some strangeness growing silently between them as they both considered the possibility of faeries and where they might live, and the mystery of the burnt logs, imagined the revels that must have happened in this odd hollow place. Sheryl stared at the charred fire pit and saw faces writ there in the remains, orange faces, elliptical by firelight, whispering.

August

Pomarium videre non potes propter pomos:
(You can't see the orchard for the trees.)

While in the summer place one evening, watching the sun fall into the blue abyss of Boar's Head Bay through her binoculars, Sheryl-Anne saw a Cadillac shimmering along County Road Ten. Glossy and cloud-coloured, the white car simmered along the hardtop like a mirage, divine and wicked all at once, and surprisingly, turned into the MacRae farm. Sheryl held her breath and watched as the Cadillac shuddered to a stop outside their house. A driver wearing a smart little cap hopped out and opened the door for someone inside who didn't bother to get out. Fergus appeared on the porch, descending the steps two at a time, clutching a large brown paper bag like an eager school boy, and dipping his tall body down, he slipped into the mysterious interior of the shiny Cadillac. The door shut and the gentle click of its closing echoed in the valley.

Sheryl wrapped her bony limbs around the branch to brace herself and settled down, waiting for her Uncle Fergus to step back out. She pushed away a shock of windblown hair, focussing and refocussing, trying to bring the Cadillac closer, her eyes perusing the brushed-aluminum roof and knife-edged fins, but the windows were tinted so she couldn't see inside.

The sky was purple and bruised on its edges, and the sun shrank to the size of a burnt plum. Finally, Fergus got out waving and smiling, all his teeth showing, and the Cadillac drove away. Sheryl watched as the car hovered like a dream, retreating down the road in a cloud of dust, just as mysteriously as it had come. Sheryl was nervous and thrilled: *The Mystery of the White Caddy,* she thought. She hopped down from her lookout post in the maple and rushed down the hillside, galloping through the orchard until she got to the house, where she confronted Fergus sitting on the porch with a dusty hardcover open on his lap, one hand in Eleanor's own two palms, reading while Sheryl's aunt gave him a manicure. But when she asked him who the stranger was he said only, get ready for bed, that's a girl.

The next day was like Christmas, Fergus was in the best of moods, he came home from the pharmacy at noon and brought presents for everyone: perfume for Eleanor, *Oh darling, it's l'Air du Temps, you shouldn't have*! and *Miss Chatelaine* magazines for Sheryl, a carton of Kents for Peter and for Josh a brand new G.I. Joe, the first boy doll Sheryl had ever seen. Josh jumped up and down in the kitchen, beside himself. Fergus was sporting a new haircut and grinning like a Cheshire cat. He paced the kitchen in his heavy white coat, talking non-stop about what a great summer it was turning out to be, how things were looking up, how this was the year, his year, by golly, the summer of 1964. An hour later the bulk bins arrived. They sat in the yard, reeking of spruce and pine, huge next to the small square orchard boxes, Earl boasting that each one of the suckers could hold twenty bushels. The MacRae men circled them, running their square pulpy hands over the new wood. Eammon drove out the tractor with the new Bartlett forklift mounted on back. Bulk bins were useless without a forklift, no single man could lift twenty bushels, and parked it in the yard and Jimmy Garrick whistled.

Sheryl watched from the porch railing, where she perched, finishing off the last few pages of *The Secret of Shadow Ranch*. Feeling peevish and disillusioned ever since she discovered that the phantom horse was nothing but a trick with a projector.

There was a pile of rickety orchard boxes with weathered red lettering sitting abandoned on the trailer. Suddenly she felt nostalgic for her grandparents' time when boxes were the size a man could lift, and there weren't machines for everything. It struck her that before the new game could begin the old one would have to die. Everywhere she saw proof of Fergus's convictions.

For the last few days of July the newspapers had been splattered with headlines shrieking in hysterical capitals: *NEGROES, POLICE BATTLE IN RIOT TORN WEEKEND IN ROCHESTER.* The riots had spread from Harlem earlier in the month to towns across America. In Toronto, there were demonstrations all along Yonge Street.

Underneath the American headlines there were pictures of shattered storefronts, smoke billowing out of windows, dark faces burning and looting, the ongoing protest against the shooting of a Negro boy. A man on TV said that Communist-inspired transients were responsible for the lawlessness, but a coloured man shouted: The black man is on the move! He's been downtrodden too long!

At breakfast Sheryl had asked what downtrodden meant. And Eleanor had told her: You know, it's when you do things for people all the time and they do diddly-squat for you. Sheryl thought maybe all this rioting was the beginning of the end and they were merely living in a cocoon in Eden Valley, the chaos hadn't reached them yet.

This baby can accomplish the work of four to six good men, Earl shouted from the yard. They took turns sitting in the driver's seat, lifting the empty bulk bins up and down. Fergus lifted his coffee cup and proposed a toast to the twentieth century, heck to the harvest of 1964, to man's ingenuity and the triumph of will over nature, and all the men raised their coffee cups in unison.

August was the beginning of apple season, which stretched out until November, picking up the pace in the fall months. The Red Askertons were the next to mature. They were a peculiar apple in that the trees didn't ripen all at once, but one at a time, sometimes only a basket a day, while the others remained hard and green, bauble-like. Eammon told Sheryl nature made them that way expressly for fresh family eating.

Finally the long heat wave was over, but in Eden Valley the farmers sat about the radio and listened to agriculture reports of drought further south. Summer still felt long and luxurious, and the days were dry and cool, the sun high and kinder overhead, the sky an endless blue.

Uncle Earl's abattoir got busy overnight, and trucks laden with squealing pigs and complaining cattle rumbled up and down their road. Josh played G.I. Joe for hours with Andrew Vanderboch next door, whose daddy was ill.

There was still no word about the McDonald boy and the newspaper published a picture of him asking anyone for information on his whereabouts.

There was a lull in the orchards every year around August before the flurry of picking began in September. The spraying was done and the war with apple scab had been either lost or won, and fertilizing and pruning was pretty much out of the question. The orchards smelled heavenly, the trees thick with waxy leaves and ruby-red clusters.

Sheryl spent the mornings feeding the pets and goofing around, lounging in her room chewing Double-Bubble gum and reading a new mystery Fergus had given her. *The Secret of Red Gate Farm* gave her the willies, it was about some sort of nature group called The Black Snake Colony that believed in living an outdoor life and danced in white robes by the light of the moon. Sheryl turned page after page wondering if the book would turn out to be about the faery people Fergus always talked about.

At noon the orchard work crew paused briefly, and Eleanor and Sheryl brought them lunch: egg-salad sandwiches and Kool-Aid in big pitchers that were hard to carry without spilling.

Eleanor had taken a job as an Avon lady, and she dressed up mornings now and clicked out the door with her pink makeup case in tow to go out on appointments, rushing back for an hour to serve lunch and returning again, sometimes a little tipsy, later on in the afternoon.

One morning Levon showed up in their yard. He cycled in on an old bicycle painted bright carnival colours, and leaning the bicycle against the barn he dawdled outside the house waiting for someone to find him. No one thought to investigate the barking. Peter and Eammon discovered the boy out there on their way to the barn, having a staring contest with Lupus whose yapping bothered him not one iota. Turned out Fergus had hired the deaf boy to help for a few weeks, and from that day on he was in the yard when the screen door slammed and Sheryl went to the window to watch the old John Bean tractor motor out to the orchard.

The boys picked high up in the lofty trees, almost invisible except for their feet, the grand limbs of the Askertons rustling as though a posse of squirrels were loose among them, until Levon and Peter descended with their picking baskets full and emptied them into the new bulk bins. Sheryl usually helped out for two hours around three. She loved orchard work, the quiet rhythm of manual labour on summer days while the picking was still unhurried. She did the grading, which involved snapping off the leaves and twigs and throwing out any apples that were too small or had scab or bitter pit or excessive bruising. When the bin was full, Eammon lifted it with the handy new Bartlett onto the tractor wagon.

Levon turned out to be an excellent picker. He was small and compact and nimble, he worked quickly and crashed around fearlessly in the trees and no amount of weather could discourage him. Still he was shy and would only tip his baseball cap in hello to her when he came up to the house mornings and Sheryl was sitting playing cat's cradle on the porch. She saw him speaking that strange sign language only with his friends, otherwise he stared quietly at the others while they gossipeong themselves and when she talked to him she felt her lips become bulbous and prissily important, with his eyes upon them.

Sheryl took to bringing her transistor with her afternoons and, turning it up loud, they listened to music while they picked, singing along to the songs whose words they knew. Peter sang loudest of all, the birds and crickets drowned out by their renditions of Elvis Presley, the Beatles, Herman's Hermits, the Supremes and Nat King Cole. Levon stared at them while they carried on, twirling a finger by his ear to indicate they were loony tunes. He couldn't hear the music so Sheryl flattened his hand against the transistor, and he grinned then from the vibration tickling his palm.

When the day's work was done, Levon disappeared into the bush and the MacRaes sauntered up to the main house and sat on the porch. When Fergus got home he donned his fancy gentleman's smoking jacket and pretended to be a waiter, taking orders for cocktails.

Will that be a Shirley Temple for you, Princess? he would say to Sheryl while she giggled. A half an hour later he would return with Eleanor dispensing drinks for everyone, and the whole family would sit together watching the sun retire, drinking Tom Collins and Harvey Wallbangers and concoctions made with ginger ale. Fergus entertained them with stories and anecdotes and his many opinions on everything under the sun, giving Peter his undivided attention. These days Peter got anything he wanted. Sheryl's uncle was happiest with a new friend in the house, and the troubled restless days seemed far away. She felt like one of the grownups sipping her Shirley Temple, sitting on the porch in the dusk, feeling safest before darkness fell.

One cool summer evening, after dinner, Sheryl and Josh wheeled out the blue CCM and Sheryl pedaled while Josh balanced on the handlebars. They rode all the way into town like that, the sky a sea of floating cumulus above, soaring through Cedar Hollow, cycling past the stately homes built by long-dead lumber barons and the tree-lined streets until they got to the rough side of town near the apple co-op and the canning factory and the new warehouse where they made tires. After riding around in circles, Josh saying, go left, no right, no left again, sorry, they finally found the street Harry Madeline lived on.

Stop! There it is, Josh pointed, complaining that he was permanently injured and had purple gonads from riding on the handlebars. They parked the bike across the street and ogled the ramshackle house, the porch disintegrating, the shingles blood red and dingy from wear and the windows unpainted for many years now. It was hardly more than the size of their shed at home and seemed sad and neglected, even more so because there was a stone fence all around the outside like you'd see usually around a bigger, grander house. In the yard, there were piles of stones everywhere in little tumbling towers. Sheryl examined them through her binoculars but they were as mysterious and bewildering up close.

When they got up the nerve to saunter over they leaned their elbows on the wall and gawked shamelessly at the muddy stone-filled yard. Josh said Jeff Vanderboch had seen Ralph McDonald sitting right there the day the twelve-year-old had disappeared. There'd been a complaint about a missing cat. One week before a tabby had been found dead on the property of the canning factory, its tail amputated.

I figure Harry makes kitty stew, Josh said. He sang quietly: *The worms crawl in, the worms crawl out, in your stomach and out your mouth....*

Sheryl couldn't help thinking of the missing Mississippi activists, the FBI scouring the countryside looking for them. Mrs. McDonald crying on the radio.

Will you quit with that corny worm song! she spat at Josh.

A black cat appeared whining at Harry's door and a grey one watched them from inside on a windowsill and Sheryl said, why would he hurt them if they're pets. They wouldn't hang around if he didn't treat them nice.

You never know, Josh shrugged. Cats are stupid.

They'd both hoped something more exciting would happen, had secretly even been looking for trouble, but there was nothing to do now that they were there and Harry wasn't anywhere about and Sheryl thought it shameful all of a sudden to be spying on a poor old man who was half-mad and obsessed with rubble.

What do you figure he does with all those stones? Josh asked but Sheryl didn't know.

Maybe he's trying to build a new house or a bigger wall, something big and strong to keep the world out.

Maybe, he said. He's crackers either way.

I dare you to go knock on his door, Sheryl said.

Josh ran across the road, brazenly banging on the door, then turned and ran.

A few minutes later they saw Harry's grizzled maw peek out the door.

Cat skinner! Josh yelled and they both took off.

That night, the men were working late in the orchard, and they trickled up the road after dark. Eammon went into his apartment, and Earl walked home, a screen door slammed but still Peter didn't show. Sheryl was waiting for him by the dim yellow light of the barn's single bulb, her legs like spaghetti from standing over bulk bins all day, nervous in the falling dark. They had taken to sharing a smoke together in the hayloft after Sheryl finished feeding the rabbits at night. When he didn't come she lifted her binoculars and examined the house through a chink in the wood.

Finally she saw the light in the kitchen snap on, and there he was, his billed cap against the yellow wallpaper, his cocky dimpled smile, then Eleanor's frothy beehive appeared also and they stood close, talking, too close for friends or neighbours as far as Sheryl was concerned. Their lips were moving but there was no sound and for a second Sheryl thought that this must be what Levon saw. They drifted away from the window, the kitchen light went off but Sheryl filled the darkness with jealous thoughts.

Moments later, she heard Josh out on the porch calling her into the house: Sheryl! Yoohoo, Sheerrrylll! and Sheryl shouted back through the hole in the barn wood, that she was coming, she just had to feed Lupus. Fergus had asked her to feed him this summer, and she was crabby about it, didn't know why all of a sudden it had to be her job. She had noticed red, raw weeping sores on Lupus's hind legs from hurling his behind through the dirt defending his territory, and she was shocked by how he was the instrument of his own suffering.

Sheryl collected the dog's slop pail but when she got outside she heard a growl in the darkness.

Her red-haired cousin crouched in pyjamas, a cottony white ghost in the dusk, just outside Lupus's circle. He was running a stick back and forth in the dirt not far from Lupus's nose, teasing him, and the dog's growl came from somewhere deep in his throat.

Quit it, Sheryl said, but Josh ignored her and kept dragging the stick through the dirt. Sheryl put the food by Lupus's dog house, and he lunged at her in an explosion of barking that knocked both her and Josh backwards into the grass.

Now you've done it, Sheryl scolded, wrestling the stick from her cousin. The food had been spilled and there was no help for it. The white mongrel was still choking himself, leaping at the boy.

You shouldn't tease him, Sheryl said. He could bite your head off. They walked up to the house, Josh shuffling beside her, obnoxious and sleepy.

A car turned in the drive, and Jimmy Garrick from the abattoir pulled up. As he got out, Fergus rose wearily from the porch swing putting his book and pencil aside. The two children joined him and stood for a moment on the steps watching Jimmy approach, Lupus still barking.

Crazy mutt, Jimmy said. I don't know why you keep him, Fergus. Are you sure he doesn't have rabies? He's mad as a hatter, that one.

Good watchdog though, Fergus said. He barks at everything that moves.

Oh, I don't know how good that is. He just about took off Sheryl's arm. I was watching from the road as I come in.

Josh was teasing him.

I was only playing, Josh said, his face pinched and irritable with fatigue. Jimmy, little Jimmy as all the grownups called him although he was big and square and old by Sheryl's standards, lifted his cap, smoothed his thinning hair and then replaced it again.

I'm no expert when it comes to dogs but aren't they supposed to be man's best friend? He regarded the yard, the grey cedar barn. Loyal they are. Dogs. Takes a lot to make them mean. I don't know what you did to this one, MacRae, but he's the meanest thing on four legs.

Two, Sheryl said.

Jimmy chuckled. She has me there.

Car accident, Fergus said smiling at Lupus. He's been crippled since he was a pup. I've been training him to be a watchdog.

Well, Jimmy said, he sure is ugly. Jimmy shook his head and seemed to think on this a while, his leg jiggling nervously as he stood there. He looked at the children. Aren't they supposed to be in bed? Fergus laughed and told Sheryl and Josh to go into the house. Josh trundled inside and Eleanor called him up to bed. Sheryl followed him reluctantly, not wanting to go upstairs and face the night. Once inside she tiptoed into the front room and squatted by the hi-fi nearest the window, flipping album covers and eavesdropping.

I'm sorry I came by this time of night.

Not to worry, Fergus clapped him on the shoulder, you come by anytime you please. I've got your package in the shed, make yourself comfortable while I go fetch it. Little Jimmy waited, pacing back and forth on the porch while Sheryl studied his mismatched shoelaces through her binoculars. He had been a tiny child, hence the nickname, but Sheryl couldn't imagine him as a boy. When Fergus got back he handed Jimmy a small brown paper bag.

Thanks a million, Jimmy said and laughed, but it wasn't a happy laugh, wasn't cheerful as a laugh ought to be.

My pleasure, Fergus said, and Sheryl saw Jimmy hand something to Fergus, which he quickly shoved into his pocket without even looking at it.

I wouldn't, except that last lot you gave me really helped. I get so nervous, there are so many worries now what with the new business and another baby coming ....

No explanation necessary, Fergus said waving him off. Just don't breathe a word or I'll have to have a little chat with your wife about this nasty new habit you're developing.

Jimmy blanched from the sting.

Fergus laughed and clapped him on the shoulder. Just testing, kiddo, he said, smiling.

They stood there a minute staring out at the darkening fields, Lupus greedily devouring his food. It was a cool night, a breeze stirred the cedars. A lone bat circled the barn. Still Jimmy didn't leave.

No word about that McDonald boy yet.

No, Fergus said. Another one lost to the big city. They usually turn up in the end, eventually.

Another cat's been found carved up too, Jimmy added. Missing an ear or something.

Probably Harry Madeline up to his crazy mischief, Fergus said. That man needs hospitalization.

Yeah. They stood, staring at the dog. Lupus was gracefully licking his white paws with long, loving strokes of his pink tongue.

Funny thing about dogs, Jimmy said, you can mistreat them a long time and they'll still love and obey you, but once they turn mean there's no fixing them. Might as well put a bullet between their eyes. I don't know about you, but that's what I would do with this one.

Sheryl lay in her pyjamas, under the starlight by the open window, cradling her transistor. On the news, the announcer said that three North Vietnamese boats had fired torpedoes at a U.S. destroyer in the Tonkin Gulf. In reply, U.S. aircraft had dropped bombs on North Vietnamese bases. She wasn't sure what it all meant but the word bomb conjured scary television images of the big one, the atomic bomb with its mushroom cloud, the end of the world.

Hey, how about them reds? Dr. Beat joked. Built your bomb shelter yet? There's trouble heating up out there folks. Good thing it's all peaceful here in Ontario tonight. Stay tuned we've got another half-hour of rock-a-bye music from the top forty for ya ...

Sheryl went out walking alone the next morning along the back roads, feeling miserable and sorry for herself, when an old car pulled up alongside. She saw the faces of a few boys, strangers all, and they whistled at her and then said to one another loud enough so she could hear, Hey, it's that MacRae girl, and she said, Hello, how are you? Politely. They chortled wickedly and said: Aren't you a sight for sore eyes? How about giving us a little squeeze of those titties? and Sheryl's face flushed hot as the flirtation turned menacing.

Leave me alone, she said, suddenly realizing she *was* alone and on a country road no less.

How's your mother? they called out cruelly. Remember the family that lays together stays together! they sniggered, and Sheryl ran then. The car squealed off after her, and looking back she saw it hit the gravel. She fell, rolling into the ditch, scraping her knee, but picked herself up without losing a beat, and ran across a farmer's field without looking back.

She ran through corn and wheat, tall and waving in the wind, dotted with butterflies and yellow jackets, over gofer holes and muddy tractor ruts, the day warm and perfect, tufted clouds scuttling the sky overhead. She ran terrified, not thinking about anything or how many miles she'd have to run across the meadows, past the new development's dirt hills, bulldozers and billboards, and on out to the highway again in order to get home. She just ran and ran like a wild horse the way she did as a kid until she ran plum out of breath on the other side of the development and collapsed, gasping and holding her knees, staring at the dust on her sneakers.

A truck drove up, bee hives jostling in back, the white and silver supers piled high, the dust from the truck's tires flying up and blinding her. Seeing her panting there by the side of the road, the beekeeper had the kindness to pull over and ask if she needed a lift. She stared hard at the buzzing hives, her head cocked to one side and asked if they'd sting her. He said not unless she bit them first. He had a kind face and she had a ways to go yet so she said, Yes, sir, thank you sir, and climbed on in.

The Supremes were playing on the radio, singing, "Baby Love," her favourite song, while two big furry dice hung from the rear-view mirror, swinging back and forth as though to keep time with the music, and Sheryl admired the shiny leather seats on the man's new truck.

Brand new, yessirree, he told her, then he asked what in the dickens was she doing running down the road in the middle of a summer day. I wasn't feeling myself, she said and took the barrette out of her hair,

letting the sable mess shake forward and conceal her from the mean
and dusty world outside.

I'll bet you weren't, he said, but seeing as she was such a good girl
and so polite and he was going up the road anyways, he agreed to take
her as far as the next concession. Sheryl nodded and said thank you,
and sat in the seat clicking her barrette open and closed in her palm in
time to Diana Ross, making small talk and enjoying the summer breeze
whistling in her ear from the open window.

He told her his name was Bob Drecker, but she could call him Buzz
if she wanted, he winked. He was a beekeeper, brought bees every
spring to the orchards in the valley.

I never did like bees, Sheryl said, nervously looking around, there
were a few worrying the corner of the back window, and she was afraid
they might get in.

I always run whenever one comes near. My auntie says I have a
regular phobia about them. Does it hurt when they sting you? she asked
and he winked.

Not if you swear a lot.

They drove past the fields, a roadside stall selling peaches and field
tomatoes, the beekeeper making idle chit-chat. The tires kicked up
stones and dirt, as they motored along, protected from the world in
their own dust cloud.

Yeah, it's been a marvelous year for bees, super year for honey, he
said. We've been lucky with those two big rains in spring, the clover
came into bloom twice this year. Hot though for a while there.

Sheryl clicked her barrette a few dozen times and told him her name
was Sheryl-Anne and her uncles owned MacRae Brothers' Orchards.

Do they now, he said. I knew your grandfather, Arthur MacRae.
Course, he's gone now. Do you remember him?

Hardly, sir.

Well, no harm done. Between you and me and the lamppost he was
an odd fella, Drecker chuckled, adding, don't tell nobody I said so.

No, sir, Sheryl smiled.

All kinds of stories went round about the strange goings-on up at
the MacRae farm. Bad-apple MacRae they called him. Half-cut every
Saturday. Parties at odd hours. The house all lit up and picnics any time
of the day and night.

 Buzz whistled and slapped the steering wheel gleefully.

Of course, people love to tell stories, and you never know which
half is true and which half is entertainment. It's always best to mind
your own beeswax, he chuckled, isn't that right?

Yes, sir. Sheryl checked the window again to make sure the bees hadn't found a way to get in.

There was a magazine on the front seat and Buzz passed it to her and told her to have a look. On the cover was a man whose face was covered with bees and she gasped horrified, feeling creepy crawly all over.

That's called a bee beard, Drecker said, ever seen one of them?

She told him she hadn't and he explained that they covered themselves in honey water and then put drones—the male bees without stingers-on themselves, and the drones crawled around licking up all the honey. It was a thing they did at fairs, bee beards, he told her.

Sheryl stared at the photo, it gave her the shivers the sight of all those bees stingless or not, and she scratched idly at her shin. She wanted to ask him more questions about the photo but couldn't form them in her mind somehow, the pictures were coming again, and she could hear a voice inside her head: *This is what happens to little girls who snitch.*

Sheryl wrestled with the door handle, trying to open it, panicking, her breath ragged, but Buzz said, Take it easy partner, we're almost home, and patted her hand. Then Bob Dylan was on the radio singing, "Times They Are A-Changin,'" and his voice was whiney as a child's with a bad cold, but still there was something fresh and haunting about that voice, it sounded strangely like everything that was changing in the world and Sheryl calmed down. She turned to Drecker and said she knew someone who could play that song and he said, Do ya now? Then they were at the farm and Buzz was saying, Out you go. Be a good girl.

When she got to the farm Sheryl felt suddenly guilt-ridden for having run off all morning. A wagon of bulk bins stood in the yard full of apples, but there was no one in sight. She heard hammering in the barn and went to see what was happening. She peeked through the door and saw Peter, his shirt off, sweat dripping down his thin back, looking small and insubstantial, an unlikely hero or protector next to the wicked boys out on the road.

Still the sight of him, quietly whistling, was a welcome one and she felt forgiving suddenly, spurred on by her near escape and newfound powers as a girl with admirers, a girl who was tormented by boys, even evil ones, and better still, got away from them.

Hey Angelo! she called out to him, calling him by the nickname the men always used, and he started, dropping the hammer in surprise.

Hey, Sheryl, he mumbled. He was fixing a picking pail. One strap had come loose and was dangling in his hands, and he was fastening it when she entered the barn. He went back to his work, not looking at her, as though shy all of a sudden.

Where's Eammon?

Orchard, Peter said.

She leaned against the barn wall and watched him.

What happened? he said going back to his hammering.

Nothing.

Your knee, he pointed with the hammer's end.

Sheryl looked down and saw blood from the gash on her knee.

Fell, she said and spit on her finger and began rubbing at her shin, smelling the earthy stink of blood and spit mingled together.

We missed you at lunch, he said, playin' hooky?

Yeah, I went for a walk, she answered. I waited for you in the barn last night, but you didn't come, she blurted out.

He looked at his hands. Sorry, I couldn't get away, he muttered, not sounding sorry at all.

She was quiet, afraid to outright ask him about Eleanor, listening to barn swallows swooping in and out of the open windows. Finally she asked him if he wanted to go for a walk with her seeing as it was such a nice day, warm but not too hot and summer wouldn't last forever, seeing as she wasn't doing anything and he wasn't doing much of anything either, far as she could tell.

He seemed to think about that for a while. Eammon was busy in the orchard tying spreaders to the small dwarf Spys to keep their limbs from growing too close together. The Red Askertons and Melbas were almost finished, and Peter needed a break and wouldn't be expected back for awhile, he said. He agreed to go soon as he got the basket fixed, which he did promptly while Sheryl went into the storage room and helped herself to a flask of Earl's dandelion wine.

They walked up the hill through long grass with clumps of timothy and goldenrod, stopping to share a smoke together, sitting in the tall yellow-green plants listening to the wind rustling. When they finished the cigarette they climbed the hill and walked along the red-shale ridge of the escarpment, where the world was gnarled and damp and threatened to pitch itself forwards into the valley below.

They walked to the summer place and stood a moment looking down at the view of the farm and the house, the valley and the town shining in the sunlight below. Earl and Jimmy Garrick's slaughterhouse was across the road, the doomed animals lowing from their stalls; the horizon hazy and unknowable.

When they tired of looking, Sheryl and Peter pursued the meandering stream down past the hidden waterfall. They traversed a dense and light-filled forest full of maples and elms, dogwood and silver birch that miraculously opened into a clearing with a small pond. The water was clean and still, revealing small tricky fish darting across a sandy bottom.

This is Petun Pond, Sheryl said. The Indians used to come here to swim. They lived in the caves up on the escarpment.

They stood staring at water sliders doing the breast stroke across the water's dusky surface. Sheryl got out the flask and passed it to him, and they took turns swilling the warm sweet wine. The pond seemed to glow, to grow safe and warm and dreamy from the fermented dandelions in her blood.

Wanna go swimming? she asked him. I don't have to be in the orchard until three.

Nah, he said and sat down to smoke again, and Sheryl looked at him a minute and smiled and shrugged and said: Oh well, I think I will.

Suit yourself, he said and she said, I will, and she began to strip then, her back to him, feeling surprised at herself, knowing he was surprised too even though he said nothing, didn't dare say, maybe you better keep your clothes on.

While she undid the buttons of her blouse she felt how the dandelion wine made her bold. She heard a crow caw and the wind start up in the trees and she thought of how she and Peter were alone and far away from everything she'd known, on a stolen afternoon where all the rules were made to be broken.

The sun was hot on her skin and she felt eager to hold summer a little longer, afraid as she was of what would happen once harvest was over, tormented by the idea of him moving on. Her uncle had said she should make him feel at home, so why stand on ceremony? She stripped herself naked starting with the blouse with the Peter Pan collar and then her new white Playtex brassiere that said double A on it, working on down until she had dropped everything but her underpants, which she hesitated to take off and in the end decided to leave on.

All the time she could feel his eyes upon her like the warm air on her skin, but she wasn't afraid. She wasn't afraid of him like she was of other boys, she didn't know why. Whether it was because he was as pretty as a girl; because he was polite and said yes, sir and no, sir and looked like Jimmy Dean; or because he was a runaway and therefore almost an orphan like herself; or perhaps because her Uncle Fergus had brought him home to be her friend; or even because right now she was a little tipsy if all was said and done and the pond swam in a glorious blur before her eyes. Maybe because of all these things, she wasn't afraid of him watching. She liked knowing he was looking at her, unable to look away. It felt as close as talking, like telling secrets without saying anything at all.

She waded into the warm water slowly, first her feet and then her knees and then her thighs. It was delicious to be naked and wet, to be a girl with a boy by a pond in the middle of the afternoon in summer. She thought about the joys of having skin and how it was like kissing entering water. French kissing. The only thing you could really compare it to was kissing.

She dove in and swam back and forth across the little pond a couple of times, floating on her back and watching the small pink islands her breasts made above water, knowing he too was looking at them, calling out to him the funny shapes the clouds made in the sky: I see a tree, a rabbit, a tractor, a boy by the water.

And he called back: I see a tractor, a Corvette, and a naked girl in the water. Oh no, I change that, eh, she's still got her panties on.

Sheryl laughed and dove down deep to touch the bottom but it was a murky and reed-infested other world, and she came back up before reaching sand. She did the dog paddle, her underpants ballooning like a homemade life preserver of white cotton, but she missed him and maybe he missed her too because he called out to her: Is it cold?

No, not a bit, she assured him, adding, Why don't you check it out for yourself, and he did, stripping naked in front of her. She watched him, noticing the chicken skinniness of his legs, the fine gold hair all over him, the girly waist. She saw too that his private part was at half-mast and bobbed ridiculously as he walked, and even though he pretended not to notice, he knew and she knew it was because he had been looking at her.

He dove in and swam out to her and they tread water together but apart in the greenish wet. Until, looking for some boyish excuse to touch her, he dunked her head. She pulled him in after and they went down together, the water stinging their eyes. For a moment they were suspended underwater their skin pond yellow, and she looked up at him where he floated above her his eyes closed, bubbles escaping through his nose, the sun a halo around the wet fronds of his hair, and everything was silent and still. When they burst the surface they were both spluttering and out of breath but the awkwardness was gone. He grabbed for her naked fishy self under the pretense of pushing her down under again, but this time his hands lingered over her wet skin, and his groping was obvious. She squirmed away from him and swam to the shore to lie her belly on the sand, a mermaid in white cotton panties.

He swam in too and lay next to her, the two of them warming their backs in the sun.

Sheryl swallowed some pond water, made a spout and spit it into the air. Whale spout, she said.

He drank some water and gargled with it. She laughed and shimmied closer.

Truth or dare? Sheryl said.

Okay truth.

Have you ever um, done it with a girl?

He stuttered at this, chuckling a little, You sure do ask some nosy questions, Sheryl-Anne.

You have to tell the truth, she said.

He hung his head, swallowed some water and made his own whale spout. Beluga, he said.

Truth, she said back.

Well, no, but I've done other things. Then he added: You shouldn't be talking such nonsense, nice girl like you, Slim. That's for your wedding night.

Her face grew solemn, shadowed.

Sheryl said she didn't think she was ever going to get married, she was going to become a private investigator. She turned over and lay her head in the sand so that the water lapped at her breasts and the sand gritted tickly beneath her shoulder blades, and she wondered who this rude girl was inside her who was always saying and doing things that scared the heck out of her.

My turn, she said. Dare.

Okay, he said. I dare you to show me that Frenchy kissing again, and embarrassed he added, just for practice. But before he could finish she leaned forward and kissed him hard on the lips, throwing her arms around his neck to hold him still. Then she pulled away, and they were both quiet for a minute listening to their hearts quicken.

Fergus decided they would have a hootenanny down at Kitchenhenge Sunday night complete with a bonfire and marshmallows. Peter would hold a concert for them all, play his favourite songs so that he could get used to performing in front of an audience. Fergus had already taken Peter's portrait for his first album cover. It was a glossy black-and-white head shot of Peter with his hair combed forward like Paul McCartney, a bandana around his neck, shoulders bare; Peter unsmiling, staring off into space like someone with deep and important thoughts. Fergus had framed the photograph and it sat on the living room mantel now where they all oohed and ahed at Peter the folkie regularly and told him he'd be as famous as Pat Boone or Bob Dylan one day for sure. Fergus shook his head and said as a photographer he'd seen a lot of faces but Peter Angelo had star quality, and the boy smiled.

Everyone except Earl dressed up for the party. Fergus kept two boxes of costumes he'd collected from Salvation Army stores, and Eleanor and April and Sheryl were stuffed into long flowing crepe gowns with velvet jackets like bridesmaids at a 1950s wedding, while Josh slipped on corduroy knickerbockers which he hated, and Peter dressed in a black turtleneck, a bona fide Dutch boy cap perched on his head like Bob Dylan. Fergus was the most smashing, sporting full Highland dress with a kilt and a tartan jacket and socks. Eammon wore the tam so they would match and a vest, his arms naked in the cool night air.

As dusk fell, Sheryl and Josh pressed in close to the fire to keep warm, Josh wrapped in his sleeping bag like a mummy, roasted marshmallows in the waning light while the adults sipped wine and chatted among themselves. Peter played just about every campfire song they knew and a few Beatles songs too, and they all joined in on the chorus, clapping loudly when the song was over.

The wine launched Fergus into one of his preachy moods and he stood up before them, kilt fluttering.

In the time to come, pure love will rain down from heaven and join hands with pure hatred ascended from the depths of hell, he shouted.

We exist here now, but not for long. The tide has turned towards destruction, this is God's will, for it was He who created the dark forces and heaven and earth, and as we enter the latter days, the lower impulses will be unleashed to carry out God's plan in uniting the goat and the lamb.

The fire crackled. The sun was no more than a cherry glow in the purple chaos that was the horizon, and Sheryl shivered, feeling night creep closer. Sheryl's long-winded uncle told them all to take a moment to meditate silently on the coming of the end and how they might prepare themselves and Sheryl stared hard at the flames until her eyes hurt. She didn't always know what Fergus was on about but didn't want to say anything.

Like the early Christians, we have to be willing to make sacrifices for the family if it is to be the protective tribe we all secretly want, he said. We have to risk more, he raved, give up our attachments to comfort, to fear, to the body, but most of all, to mortal and corrupt ideas of right and wrong.

There was a pause, and they all nodded, sitting quietly, cross-legged and attentive, and Sheryl worried about what sort of things she might have to give up. April blew her nose and wiped her eyes and Sheryl wondered if she was crying. So be it, Fergus said, and Eammon and Earl said, As it is.

There are two doorways to God, Fergus continued, adjusting his glasses, running a delicate hand through his crow-coloured hair, summoning patience for the undisciplined rabble assembled before him.

Religion is like a house with two doors. Strangers use the front door but people who are familiar with the house use the back. We can teach you things, kiddo, Fergus turned to Peter then, the back door, the secret passage, but you have to be willing....

I'm cool, Peter said, and Sheryl disliked him in that moment. She thought he would jump in a lake if Fergus said so.

Betrayal is too close to the MacRae blood, we've known betrayal and in the bloodline it is worse, Fergus said, looking straight at Sheryl and she toyed with her shoelaces, sure he could only mean her mother.

But blood itself—now there's something—blood *is* life, Fergus ranted on, the firelight reflected in his glasses. By sharing our blood we become brothers and sisters not just on this earth but on the spiritual plane, which is vital in the Now and will be even more so in the time to come.

At this he produced a knife from a sheath at his belt buckle and cut his thumb. He stressed that no one repeat what happened here tonight and everyone promised. Then he took Peter's left hand and made a small slice there while the boy gasped in surprise. Fergus christened him Angel Boy and, pressing their bleeding thumbs together, he said Peter was now the fourth horseman. Holding their bloody thumbs up he announced they were blood brothers, and there could be no betrayal among them. The others clapped and hooted, stamping their feet in rhythm, and Fergus had everyone pick a partner to become blood brothers or sisters with. So Josh and Sheryl cut each other's index fingers, Josh tired and whining, I mean don't we already have each other's blood? We're related, right? Sheryl scolded him and told him to do as he was told or he'd get them into trouble.

Afterwards, Eleanor took Josh off to bed. Sparks flew up into the starry sepulchre. Sheryl stared at the appliances out in the meadow glowing bone-white in the moonlight, and was struck by how ordinary things became so disturbing at night.

Peter played "Puff the Magic Dragon" and they all sang along, clapping their wounded hands and singing while Fergus passed around a container of Pez candies for the adults. Sheryl asked if she could have one but her uncle said no and told her she could stay only if she lay down and was quiet. He offered her some warm dandelion wine to help her sleep, which gave her the hiccups. She curled up in Josh's sleeping bag by the fire while the adults smoked and talked and giggled together for what seemed like hours. Sheryl awakened once to drunken singing and when no one was looking she pocketed the Pez by the picnic cooler not far from her. Huddling in her sleeping bag she ate one of the candies, which wasn't a candy at all but a little piece of paper. It tasted bitter and starchy with the texture of newsprint, and she lay gazing up at the stars until sleep came to claim her once more.

She dreams the earth is breathing. The sky and stars, the trees and brush are inhaling, exhaling. Everything is alive, water, dirt, stones and fire. In the distance, torches dance through an open field of cornflowers and Queen Anne's lace. The torches thunder as they burn, roaring like a fire-breathing waterfall.

A boy is there. Spirals painted on his wrists and ankles. He is stripped to the waist in the cool night air and wears a worm-eaten fur, a torch in his hand, a set of antlers on his head. There is a fox stole around his neck, and the dead eyes stare glassy and dark.

The torches circle and bob swarming him. His torch is stolen. His clothes are torn. He rises naked and shimmering, his thin body silver in starlight. He runs silently chasing the torchlight through the field. The game is won when he has recaptured the torch, which he finally does. He stands now one foot on the panting body, holding the taper high. A wild boy, naked and triumphant, howling like a wolf.

Time yawns and spreads its jaws open. The girl's hands are white doves that twitter and rise. Her teeth hurt. She giggles uncontrollably for no reason.

Inside the barn there is the stench of blood and urine and shit. The faery king stands naked and wild.

Fuck the faery queen, fuck the faery queen! they chant and the girl runs out into the night, bare feet swallowing dirt.

Sheryl awakened to the lonely moan of the tractor in the orchard. She had a stomachache and her teeth hurt. Lifting her head, she saw the room spin. The house was quiet. Everyone had gone.

She languished in bed all morning, unable to budge, reading *The Secret of Red Gate Farm* and listening to her radio. The bodies of the missing civil rights activists had been found. The announcer said they'd been murdered and tossed in a dam full of rattlers and water moccasins.

Sheryl cried into her pillow, unsure why, except that the world seemed ugly and unfair.

After she recovered she decided to play detective to cheer herself up. Dressing up in an old trench coat of Eleanor's and green high heels, she skulked around corners, confronting imaginary intruders in the hall, examining every little thing up close through Fergus's magnifying glass, the minutiae of the world jumping bulbous and absurd under its lens.

She snooped among the books Fergus kept by his eggplant easy-chair. *Magick in Theory and Practice* by Mr. Aleister Crowley, *The Prophecies of Nostradamus*, *The Complete Pharmacy*, and a book by that man Timothy Leary. At noon Eleanor still had not returned and Sheryl went out onto the porch and stumbled over Fergus's black medical bag. Inside, there was a small arsenal of beer-bottle brown containers all with official white labels. She tried saying the names out loud: Benzedrine, Paregoric, Demerol, Percodan and Pentothal, the typed labels insisting: TAKE AS DIRECTED. There were needles and two bottles of nose drops, a flurry of little slips of paper, prescriptions with strange Latin names on them. Also a tensor bandage. She unrolled the stretchy flesh-coloured fabric and as she did, a wad of bills spilled out onto the porch, five hundred dollars in all. She put her fist in her mouth to stop the sound.

When she felt better later that afternoon, she headed out to the orchard, waking along the side porch that ran along the outside of the old farm house bypassing Eammon's silent, shady quarters, sidling quietly past on her way to Niagara Block. But as soon as her shadow crossed his door it whined open in response and he called after her.

Sheryl, hey! Where do you think you're going in such a hurry?

She stopped out of respect, but kept on walking backwards, not looking at him.

I'm helping out with the Melbas.

Since when did you get so eager to help anybody?

Since never, she said stopping and poking with her shoe at a sow bug struggling through a muddy hollow in the dirt.

I want to tell Peter something, she said and bit her lip.

Well, I'm sure it can wait, Eammon said, in a surly voice, looking at her sideways. He had come out onto the porch now and sat on the banister, one stocky leg swinging. There was classical music coming from his little apartment and she could smell toast. He was eating a peanut butter sandwich and had on his work trousers. He lived in his work clothes, and she had rarely seen him out of them except when he went to church, which was only when someone died or was born.

Today he wore only an undershirt because it was warm. His arms were large and muscled, his body restless as a trapped puma she saw in a cage outside a grocery store once. Sheryl cocked her head to one side regarding him, nibbling at her thumb, staring at the tattoo on his arm of the woman on a swing and the mysterious name *Delilah*, in blue ink below. He looked undressed sitting there and she was embarrassed and said she had to get going but he smirked, leaning against the railing of the porch eating his toast and smiling crookedly.

Come over here, I want to show you something, he said.

No, you don't, she answered, but lest she sound too cheeky she changed the subject. Did it hurt?

What?

The tattoo, did it hurt?

No, just a little. I didn't cry if that's what you mean.

Did you do it on a dare in a barroom like everybody says?

No, he said. Why don't you come over here, and I'll show you up close.

'Cause I don't want to, she replied coyly and kicked a pebble into the path of the determined sow bug. I'm gonna go now, she said, not moving.

I did it for my girlfriend, he said, hooking her with this gossip. Like a rope it kept her tied there, and she hesitated, making a flat place in the dirt with her shoe waiting for the whole story. He licked some peanut butter off his palm, taking his time, enjoying himself.

I didn't know you had a girlfriend, she said.

He chuckled. Bet you didn't think anyone would go out with the likes of me. His laughter was bitter, like lemonade without sugar.

I didn't say *that.*

You didn't have to. She was just a girl I knew in high school.

Delilah, Sheryl said, conjuring the woman who might wear this name. Why didn't you marry her then?

I don't know, he shrugged, irritated. Why does it rain some days and other days it don't?

Did you love her, and she ran away with some other guy like everybody says?

A brief turbulence travelled his face.

Don't believe everything you hear, he warned. Then he calmed himself and smiled at her and she could see the gap in his mouth where his two teeth were missing and she was sure Delilah had had something to do with it. It didn't matter if he was ever nice because when he smiled and you saw his toothlessness, he looked different somehow. She didn't like him. She rubbed her arms and left the sow bug alone. Stupid sow bug. Stupid her for taking the porch route shortcut to the orchard. She had the creepy crawlies today for no good reason.

I guess I'll be going now, she said and her sneakers wandered. Don't go, he said. You best forget about your mother, Sheryl, she was trouble on wheels. She won't be coming back for you now.

Sheryl halted motionless on the lawn. Yes, she will, Sheryl said defiantly, she will come back for me, I know it.

Your mother's got troubles, Eammon added, persisting. She can't help herself. There are things that are out of her control, things you don't know about. What kind of things? Sheryl asked, squinting up at him.

Grown-up troubles.

Sheryl hesitated for a moment. Is that why she ran off?

Eammon said, Sometimes people do funny things just so's they can save themselves.

From what? She should have taken me with her.

Maybe she figured you'd be better off without her.

Well, I'm not, Sheryl said, pouting. I'll be going now...

No wait, I have something for you. It's a present.

A present? she paused.

You'll like it. Come see.

Sheryl crossed her arms, her legs shivery, it was chill in the shade of the porch. With a sorry look behind her, she trudged up the steps and followed him.

Eammon's apartment had been built by all three brothers for their parents with the idea that as Sheryl's Grandma and Grandpa MacRae got older they would live in these quarters close by their children and be properly taken care of in their dotage, but they had died quite quickly one after the other. The apartment had its own kitchen and a glassed-in porch, as well as a small living room and a bedroom looking out onto the orchard.

Sheryl stepped inside the whinging screen door and waited for her eyes to adjust to the absence of light. The living room beyond was dark as a cave and stuffed to the rafters with odds and ends of machinery and plants growing in little pots along the windowsill and records without their covers on. She lingered by the door. It was more interesting than she'd thought his apartment might be. There was music on the radio, something classical and very grown up. Even though Eammon was rough around the edges, he always had music on, and sometimes Sheryl could hear opera coming out of his windows at night.

Somehow, she confused it with him and wondered what he was doing inside there, all that stormy singing escaping from the yellow-lit squares of windows.

Sheryl had never been inside his place before. There were plants everywhere, the little porch was like a greenhouse, alive with flowering vines and violets in pottery jars, small sprouty things in pots with names she didn't recognize. Eammon liked exotic plants. The room was close and humid and warm. She snooped, reading the occasional name tag and touching all the fronds and seedlings with wandering hands. Stopping at a white bucket where a plant with a long creeping, leafy stem leaned on a stick with bell-shaped, dark purple flowers. She lifted her binoculars to examine it up close and the plant jumped out at her, monstrous and alive.

What's this one called? she asked.

Deadly nightshade, he said, belladonna. If you eat too much of that it'll paralyze you, your body will go to sleep and you won't be able to move a bit, but you'll still be alive. It's poison.

Oh, Sheryl said. So why do you grow it?

He chuckled. I like the flowers.

He disappeared into the bedroom while she lingered by the door worrying a mosquito bite and picking at her fingers. She put fresh Band-Aids on her thumbs in the mornings now just so that she would remember to leave them alone.

He emerged from the bedroom holding a little pink box with a handle. Sheryl carefully placed her present down on the floor and opened it up. It was a portable record player. There was a turntable with a tiny needle, everything small and compact and on the outside the words: RCA Victor. Her jaw dropped. The record player was beautiful, one of the most wondrous things she'd ever seen. He knelt down beside her, balancing on his haunches so that she could smell his peanut-butter breath emerging from the threatening gap between his teeth. His eyes were feverish as he stared into hers and said: I wanted you to have it. It's for you, Slim, because you're special.

Sheryl shot up, suddenly cold and snapped the portable record player closed, hefting the thing to her and talking faster than her feet could move. She mumbled, Well, then thanks, Uncle Eammon, thanks a lot, I better be going ... Backing out of the apartment, she turned and thumped along the cedar porch, the record player slapping against her legs, and she ran like that, thumping and slapping, until she was lost in the quiet safety of the rows and rows of Talman Sweets and Rhode Island Greenings, Melbas and McIntoshes.

It rained that Sunday after church. Sheryl had kept her eyes closed the whole time so that she wouldn't look at the stained-glass windows, until thankfully the service was over, and the family spilled out onto the steps of Grace Anglican. Huddling under umbrellas by the billboard that read: Give Every Day to Christ for it Might be YOUR LAST!

The weather was fetid and warm, the July heat had returned. Once home they put on their shorts while the mosquitoes staged a comeback, swarming in miniature frenzied tornadoes by the porch where the family camped, restless and irritable.

The Sunday drive was put off due to rain, so Sheryl made gingerale floats. April and Earl weren't coming over for Sunday dinner either. Sheryl was secretly relieved, there would be no party out on the porch. It was like when school got cancelled because of snow.

Josh played with his action figure, turning the verandah into a war zone. Fergus disappeared to his darkroom downstairs, and Eleanor lay like Cleopatra on the porch swing, nursing a Bloody Mary, which Josh called a "hairy dog," a bag of frozen peas on her head and dark sunglasses on. Shrieking every time someone went in and out of the house: Don't slam the goddamn door!

Sheryl nestled into the rocking chair to read *The Secret of Red Gate Farm*. It turned out that the Black Snake Colony weren't kookie naturists but counterfeiters and strangely she was disappointed. That wasn't how the story was supposed to end, she thought. Still reading calmed her. Nancy was like an imaginary friend. Outside, rain splattered and hissed in the grass and Sheryl felt safe in the cocoon of the porch. She turned a page then, and a little piece of paper fluttered to the floor. On it was written the numbers: 11: 11. The numbers on the wall of the old barn loomed large. Her palms went damp. She shoved the paper into the pocket of her shorts.

On the inside cover her mother had scrawled, *This book belongs to Mimi MacRae* in pencil, the letters bulky and childish. Mimi. Sheryl whispered the name quietly to herself. Mimi, Mimi, mommy. Mimi grew up where Sheryl was growing up in the old farm house, with the orchards all around. Maybe Mimi had spent damp days reading on the porch. Maybe Mimi had been afraid, had dreamed of running away from home just like Sheryl did. Had run in fact, as Eammon said, to save herself.

Tonight we're going to have a really big sheyow ... The rain had stopped, and the television was on. Ed Sullivan's voice could be heard through the house. Sheryl escaped the smoky-blue sea of TV land, where the family sat mesmerized by the weekly plate spinners and acrobats, and went up to her room, shutting Sunday out.

She had found an old apple carton in the barn that said *Smiley Brothers* on the side, from the local canning factory, and she covered the carton with a small tablecloth and placed her treasure–the pink RCA Victor–on the little makeshift table. She ran her small hand over the nubbly pink and white cover of the turntable then sat down and looked at it for a long time, wondering if she'd have to be nice to Eammon now.

Knock, knock. Who's there? There was a noise coming from the closet. The girl tiptoed over and opened the door. A small child stood there, only her bare feet showing, her body stuffed inside a severed horse's head, blood pooling in a black puddle on the floor.

It was eleven past eleven when Sheryl opened her eyes. She smelled smoke and she shuddered. She crept to her window and saw a light on in the barn. Tossing her blue windbreaker over her nightgown, she drifted out into the darkness to investigate, barefoot. Lupus watching her with mongrel eyes from his dog house. Shshshsh, she said to him, and he groaned, the groan becoming a yawn, but he didn't bark.

Sheryl slipped inside the barn and heard voices. She paused, white moths hurling themselves at the lone light bulb. She wasn't cold but couldn't stop trembling.

She followed the voices, shrinking against the wall, inching along until, outside the storage room, her hand found a chink in the wood and she pressed her eye to it.

Inside she saw Eleanor and Peter half-naked lounging in their underwear on an Oriental rug in a circle of blinding light. Eleanor's with platinum hair floated outwards from her face, her large breasts drifted into her armpits under her creamy-coloured slip, her skin was so white that she seemed to glow. Peter lay on his side, stroking her thigh.

Sheryl heard Fergus's voice: Okay, that's good, smile, followed by the click, click of a camera.

In the morning, Eden Valley was enveloped in mist. The temperature had dropped, and it was suddenly cool. The maples and cedars sprouted out of the fog, floating unmoored and strange.

Sheryl shuffled outside to feed Lupus and the rabbits, finding it hard to wake up. The dog was waiting for her when she got to the old riding ring. He had begun to anticipate her. Every time she went to feed him she found him facing in her direction, and several times when she thought of him and looked out her window he would be watching her. It was unnerving.

Inside the barn, swallows scattered and Sheryl stumbled about her chores like a sleepwalker, going from cage to cage, some strange numbness upon her, as she poured pellets for the rabbits and collected Lupus's kibble.

She dragged the dog's bowl out of his circle with a stick while his white ears flattened against his head and his black lips curled. He was ghostly in the fog. Filthy too, she realized when she got closer, he had an unhealthy smell about him. She had half a mind to turn the hose on him. She filled his saucer with canned dog food and old meat loaf, and pushed the bowl back into the old riding ring keeping as far away from him as she could. But Lupus didn't lunge at her this morning. He was still and waited patiently for his food, even his growl seemed half-hearted, and Sheryl wondered if he was spooked by the fog, or finally growing used to her.

The women made apple sauces and pies all week long to sell at Goldman's Grocers: Dutch apple, cinnamon apple, apple-pork pie, apple jelly, apple mint sauce, Scottish Squares, applesauce cake, cheesecake and bread. April had come over with recipes and organized Eleanor and Sheryl, a coloured band holding her bobbed auburn hair back from her thin face, her large apron covered in flour and apple stains. Sheryl noticed that her auntie was looking more robust these days. But by accident Sheryl walked in on her in the bathroom, and discovered her sitting on the edge of the claw-foot tub crying into her apron.

Eleanor shooed Sheryl out to the barn to get packing boxes. Sheryl found Peter washing up by the sink inside the tractor room. He was singing as she came in, wetting down his hair and grinning at himself in the mirror.

Oh, it's just you, he said, when he turned and saw her, then went back to his grooming.

How could you? she spit at him.

What? he said, not looking at her, running the water over the teeth of his comb.

How could you do that with Eleanor?

Do what?

In the barn?

He blushed and told her to stop being such a nosy parker.

She frowned. I thought you were my friend.

We were just taking pictures for the album cover, he said bristling, so that I can get an agent. We didn't do anything.

Sure you didn't, Sheryl pouted, but Peter just shrugged. She went to get her secret can, lit them both a cigarette and stood slouching against the washtub.

I thought I was your girl, she said.

He pinched her cheek and said, Catch me in a few years, but when she frowned, he said, You are my girl, Slim. You and me, we're like brother and sister. We were just making pictures, for my trip to the big city. All these things take money.

She tugged on her ponytail, unsure of whether to believe him. He seemed so good and clean, freshly shaved, hair glistening, his face tanned and hazel eyes smiling. Even when he had circles under his eyes from lack of sleep and he was streaked with sweat and filthy from working in the orchard, even when he was cobweb grey from hootenannying Saturday and Sunday nights with her uncles, he was still radiant, more beautiful than anyone else in Eden Valley. She picked at the frayed Band-Aid on her bloody thumb, finished her cigarette, she couldn't be mad at him for very long.

She told him last night she'd had a nightmare about a horse, and in the dream there'd been a puddle of black water. She'd dreamt of black water before and every time she did someone died or something bad happened. She had a bad feeling.

Sometimes when I wake up in the night it feels like someone is in my room, she said, I can smell smoke, but I look around and no one is there.

You're an odd one, Slim, he said, and went back to his fiddling. I'm so tired, man, he whined, I can't move my hands. He lifted them to show Sheryl his fingers criss-crossed with little cuts, palms calloused and red, the fingernails lined with grime. They settled into a gesture of clawed surrender.

This orchard work is killing me, man.

They heard Lupus outside, first the rustle of his chain then his crazy go-for-broke barking, as he grew desperate to sink his teeth into the intruder. They went to the barn wall and squished their faces up to the small window by the rabbits' cages. The white Cadillac was slinking up their drive again slow and sleek, smoke trailing quietly from its rear, engine purring.

Well, will you get a load of that, Peter said. Who do you figure that could be?

Someone important, Sheryl said. I've seen him here once before. But he never gets out of the car. He's the mystery man. It's *The Mystery of the White Cadillac*. You wait, Uncle Fergus will get in with him, and they'll have a little chat.

Sure enough, moments later Fergus appeared on the porch holding a large brown bag wearing a big toothy grin. The car came to a halt before the house, and the driver got out and opened the back door and Fergus got in. The two teenagers craned to see the face in the back, but all they could make out was a felt hat. Fergus chatted with the man for about ten minutes, the car's engine still running, and in all that time Lupus didn't let up his crazy yapping, flinging himself against the length of his tether like a maddened creature, barking himself hoarse. Josh came out and threw a broom at him but still he wouldn't stop. Peter stood close to Sheryl and she could smell Fergus's aftershave on his skin.

What do you figure is in that brown bag? Sheryl whispered.

I don't know, he whispered back.

Just then Fergus emerged from the car and saluted the hatted figure inside. He was minus the brown paper bag and was shoving something into his wallet. Suddenly Sheryl thought that she didn't know her uncle as well as she'd once thought. He was nervous, she noticed, his hands jittery.

Money, Sheryl thought out loud. The man in the hat must be giving him money for something.

Dope maybe, Peter suggested, chuckling, what a guy.

Is Benzedrine an antihistamine? she asked Peter.

What? Hell no, Peter said, it's an upper, a pep pill, keeps you goin.' He reached into the pocket of his overalls and produced a few capsules to show her.

Your Uncle Fergus was good enough to give me these to take in the morning to get my day started. He said they would provide just the zing I need to make it through summer and harvest. I've tried a couple when I've been bagged after a heavy night, eh, and they really do the trick.

They looked just like Fergus's antihistamines. Grim pictures surfaced in her thoughts again, they wouldn't go away or leave her be.

Let's run away, she blurted out suddenly, surprising herself. I've got money saved, and I know where I can get more. Lots more. We could get on a bus to Toronto and no one would ever know. Take me with you when you go, Sheryl pleaded, throwing her arms around him and burying her face in his shoulder. I won't be any trouble.

Peter tried to pry her arms away.

Slim, you're too young, man, you're not yet fifteen. The fucking Mounties would be out looking for me. They would arrest me for kidnapping.

Sheryl felt her hopes fizzle. There would be no boyfriend, no running away, no finding her mother's house, no house with the horse's-head door knocker on it. She started to sniffle. I'll die if I stay here.

Oh come on, Slim, you're being dramatic, this is not cool, he said, wrestling free. You could get me thrown in jail.

You do other things that could get you thrown in jail, but you don't care about them, she cried into her bandaged hands, hiccuping like a small child. She was having one of her hairy fits again she knew, but she couldn't stop herself.

Peter patted her thin back.

Please, she begged between hiccups. She gave him a kiss on the cheek, then another and another.

Peter held her still. He said it was just her ego getting her down. Life was an illusion, death was life and life was death. She was stuck in the old game and had to let go, all the rules were made to be broken, and she had to stop taking life so serious.

Hearing Fergus's words come out of his mouth was unbearable, and she cried even harder, inconsolable.

All right, all right, he said, finally. I can't stand to watch a girl cry, calm down. Maybe you can come with me. Anyway, I'll think about it, he relented, just not right now, we've got to get all those apples in first. Man, am I sick of apples.

She looked up, wiping away the tears with the back of her hand. Hiccuped again.

You will take me to Toronto then? We can run away? she asked with a tentative smile. He was the most beautiful boy, the perfect boy, she embraced him and Peter sighed, surrendering: We'll see.

A few days later there were more surprise visitors. The MacRae family was assembled on the porch at the end of a working day, slurping cocktails, when a weathered truck chugged up the drive, and two local farmers got out, wearing billed caps and baggy greens, lifting tired swollen fingers to hail Fergus, followed by a nod to Eleanor and Earl. They ambled up to the porch, their eyes wary and watching her uncle the way one would watch a snake, as though Fergus were both charmed and dangerous.

The others made room for them, and Eleanor minced ladylike into the kitchen to get them all beers, still in full Avon gear of Capri pants and fake eyelashes, while they said, Don't get up, thanks we're fine here, and parked themselves on the stairs.

Sheryl recognized them both from the hardware store. They were the Hillman brothers, Sam ran the hardware store, and Arthur kept some beef cattle and a small apple orchard outside town. Hillman senior said they were in the neighbourhood and hoped the family didn't mind a friendly visit and everyone protested politely, no, not at all.

Apples coming along? Sam Hillman asked turning to Earl, eyes squinting. Askertons and Melbas all in, Earl said, Macs and Spys to go, but Eammon's on top of it. We've got Louis Venerable and his people coming to help out September.

Good enough, Sam said. Got yourself a fine new forklift there, I hear tell, enough to make people envious.

Fergus's idea, Earl clapped his brother on the back. He's the brains behind the organization.

The latest machinery, kiddo, and we're proud of her, Fergus said.

Must have cost a pretty penny?

Not too much, didn't break the bank anyhow.

Eleanor came out with a tray of beers and cocktail sausages on toothpicks.

Still no word about the McDonald kid.

Yeah, it's a sad fact, hundreds of runaways every year, Earl said.

Word going round he was last seen at Madeline's. That man is a menace and should be locked up, Fergus said.

Incurable schizophrenic, Earl added.

Crikey, Sam said. Did you hear, Mrs. Wong found her cat in the back alley in a terrible mess. Had to put it down.

What's the world coming too? Fergus said.

So who is this fella? Arthur asked Fergus, tipping his shiny bald head towards Peter.

Oh, he's the son of a relative down for the summer, Fergus lied.

Aren't you the good Samaritan.

Fergus winked. He's a good lad, helping out in the orchard until harvest is over.

Sheryl saw a dimple appear in Peter's cheek as he listened to them talk about him. He hadn't shaved, and there was a bit of stubble on his chin that only made him look more roguish and interesting.

He looks like somebody, Arthur said. Reminds me of someone. Jimmy Dean, Sheryl said, proudly.

Oh yeah, maybe that's it.

A second passed, two, three.

He's dead now, isn't he, that Jimmy Dean? the older Hillman said looking to the younger.

Eammon said, Where you been, Sam? Ask him if Kennedy's still the President of the United States.

There were nods and chuckles all round.

Car accident, Earl said, Jimmy died in a car accident years back.

Hell of a way to go.

There ain't no good way I know of, Eammon said, and all the men laughed again, but there was an edge to their laughter now.

Fergus said that Jimmy'd been driving a Porsche, a vintage 550 Spyder, and there were people who said he'd died because a curse had been put on that car.

After Jimmy had crashed, Fergus continued, the wreck went on tour across America for twenty-five cents a look, but the Spyder left nothing but calamity in its wake. First the Porsche rolled off the display and crushed a boy, a fifteen-year old Jimmy Dean lookalike, and then it fell out of the trailer, killing two more innocent bystanders, before it fell into eleven pieces in New Orleans, thank you very much.

Sheryl's uncle shook his head and adjusted his dark glasses, took a sip of his scotch. He could sound just like a farmer when he wanted to, Sheryl thought.

Finally the Porsche was put into a sealed boxcar on a train going from Florida to L.A., with two Pinkerton detectives watching over the darn thing, but wouldn't you know, when the boxcar arrives in L.A., they open the doors and there's no Spyder. Car vanished right under their noses.

The men laughed.

Well, I'll be darned, Sam said.

Truth is stranger than fiction, Fergus concluded.

Peter shook his head. Man, you know the coolest stuff.

Sheryl pulled her hands out from under her thighs. She had been sitting on them to keep herself from chewing and they had gone to sleep. Eleanor twirled her umbrella swizzle stick in her Wallbanger and told Josh to stop slurping his ginger ale.

So you got yourselves some new bulk bins I hear, Sam said, getting to the point, leaning both big hands on his knees. Farmers always wanted to talk equipment, Sheryl thought. The MacRae men nodded.

Hillman senior sucked his teeth and shook his head back and forth. Isn't that something, he continued. Last spring new shed, this summer new bulk bins, new forklift for loading the new bulk bins. Heck, you fellas must be rolling in dough.

Our folks put a little something away for us, Fergus said, smiling down at him.

A couple of the fellas seen a white Cadillac up at your place too, Sam said, while Arthur studied his lap. White Eldorado. A few jokes went around you were selling guns to the Commies or some fool thing, he chuckled, smiling through his teeth and Sheryl saw the Cadillac shimmering along the hard top like an omen. She peeked under the Band-Aid on her thumb where the skin was ragged and raw.

The MacRae brothers chuckled. Oh that, Fergus laughed, he was just looking for directions.

Twice? Sam Hillman's eyes were narrow, squinting. He crossed his arms.

Listen it's none of my business, fellas, I'm just repeating what I hear over at my place, he said, swatting away a fly.

What do you think of them new bulk bins anyhow? Arthur said, keeping the peace. Like them any better than the old orchard boxes? Me I like to stick to what's tried and true.

The conversation moved on then to more banal things: the price of apples, the excess in cold storage from last year, whether the export market was shrinking or growing, what a good season it had been, the new tire plant in town. How Wilbur one concession over was down with the cancer. Finally the Hillmans thanked Mrs. MacRae and clambered into their dusty excuse for a vehicle and drove off.

Snoopy bugger, Earl scoffed and Fergus nodded.

After church, Fergus was still not been feeling himself, he was nervous and jittery, unable to settle down. He got like that sometimes, fidgety, one leg perpetually wiggling, his hands repeatedly flying up to adjust his glasses, scratch his nose. When Fergus had a case of nerves he liked to go for a drive to calm himself. He asked Sheryl and Peter to join him around four, and as they walked out to the car, Sheryl found herself fretting about the coming darkness.

The sky was stormy and slate coloured. A big wind had come up and tossed anything small and untethered about the yard. It was hard to see for the dust blowing in her eyes. She hadn't been able to keep her thumbs out of her mouth all day and had bitten them bloody once again. Fergus's agitation only put her more on edge. The night before she had awakened twice, in the early hours it seemed the house was possessed, alive with sound.

Sheryl worried she would never sleep through the night like other people. As they reached the Bonneville, Lupus tore out of his doghouse, barking and snarling, baring his teeth and lunging at Fergus, shocking them all, and Sheryl felt her pulse in her throat.

The Bonneville circled the outskirts of Cedar Hollow aimlessly wandering, the two teenagers sitting quietly apprehensive inside the car, the day outside coming to a close, while Fergus commandeered the Pontiac through the windswept streets, talking non-stop, scanning the road as though looking for something.

Will unto love, kiddos, he said. It is only necessary to inflame the will and issue its commands, many ends, many means, to bend the astral light to the will of man. Do as thou wilt, the laws of magic are the laws of nature, and this is the science of pharmacy, of chemistry, to subdue nature to the will of man, now especially on the eve of the new age. But first we must break our links, sever our ties to the lie and dare to see reality in its awesome intensity, for there is not much time. Even now we can hear the heralds of the end, soon the whole world will quake with its coming, and we must be free by then, have broken our bonds to the human game to stand above the terror of annihilation. For after the end there is a new beginning, and we must choose-to be of the end or of the beginning. There are hints everywhere. Look at the glory around us, the fields, the farmers tending them, the bountiful crops and orchard produce, all these are the result of man's science, of man's will over nature. Many ends, many means, did I already say that? he asked glancing at Peter sitting in the passenger seat, who nodded, saying, I can dig it, that's cool.

Sheryl pondered the end. Maybe there would always be daylight in the new world, but she knew terrible things were supposed to happen first, there was Armageddon and the Four Horsemen, the earth crumbling but who could look forward to mayhem?

They drove erratically in and out of neighbouring towns for an hour or more, Sheryl's anxiety steadily mounting as she recalled all the hours she'd spent inside this car, all the years Fergus packed them up and moved their patchwork family from town to town, all the Sunday afternoons roaming endlessly, prey to his fevered restlessness. They had a home now, such as it was, some semblance of a normal life, and she was secretly worried it might all disappear. Outside the wind made the world blurry and unsettled, branches waving, stray leaves skittering across the pavement.

Finally they were circling back when they came upon Levon by the side of the road, walking his bicycle, the back tire flat, and Fergus said, Well, well, will you look at that? Opportunity knocks. Here's a chance for you youngsters to prove yourselves, he said and pulled over onto the gravel shoulder.

Mary, Mary quite contrary, he told her, ask your friend there if we can give him a lift up to the farm, help him out with his tire.

My name's Sheryl-Anne, she argued.

Then I'm asking your imaginary friend Mary to do it, Fergus insisted, and she fumed but stepped out of the car into the wild wind. Her hair streaming into her face, hands shoved into her pockets, she asked Levon if he wanted some help, and again felt his eyes focus on her mouth. He nodded, yes, and Fergus put his bicycle in the trunk and they drove back to the farm house, Fergus's hand rat-tat-tatting on the steering wheel the whole way, Peter humming along to the radio.

Once there, Peter began repairing the bicycle, which, in spite of the creative paint job, looked shoddy next to Josh's fancy CCM with its aluminum fenders and coloured streamers. Levon watched the whole procedure nervously, shuffling from side to side until Fergus told Sheryl to take him for a walk while Peter was finishing, they had time before dinner.

Without a word they set off through the cedar swamp, up the tractor road through the mixed forest, and as she was thinking of where she would take him, he picked up a discarded tree limb to use as a walking stick and bolted through the trilliums and ostrich ferns while she scrambled behind.

Gradually she could hear the sound of rushing water, and soon they were standing by a huge drainpipe that burst out of the undergrowth into the creek. The water pouring forth from its mouth had a funny smell and the pool was grimy and black-rimmed. Levon pointed at it and turned to her and she said, black water. He nodded. She wondered where this water came from, where it went, how long it would take to seep into the ground, into the wells?

They smoked a cigarette together crouching before the rude pollution. When they got back Fergus wrapped his large manicured hand around Levon's neck and steered him by the scruff, talking to him quietly, leading him towards the shed. Sheryl lollygagged in the yard among the full bulk bins, watching Fergus as he disappeared into the shed with Levon, Lupus barking his fool head off, crazy and writhing against his chain, barking and barking and more crazy barking.

That night all the MacRae family came over for Sunday dinner as usual, washed and shaved and wearing their Sunday best. Afterwards they retired to the porch for a little singsong and a few beverages. Peter pulled out Jezebel, and they lazed under the glowing bulb of the porch singing and telling jokes, Sheryl playing along while secretly keeping a lookout, one eye riveted on the silent door of the shed, Levon nowhere in sight. It was a clear cloudless night and the stars were already blinking in the sky. Sheryl had two bitter orange drinks before bed to help her sleeplessness and Lupus yapped at the porch dwellers every once in a while, still surly and excitable, while Peter scoffed, That dog is loco, man, I've never seen a dog so mental.

In the middle of the night, Sheryl sat upright in the dark, sure she'd heard crying. There was a plaintive sound on the wind, like the mewling of a kitten, *here kitty, kitty*. Within minutes, she was stealing through the grass, wrapped in her chenille bedspread, like a moth drawn to a flame, thinking how it would be lovely out in the yard in daytime, but somehow at night the world was changed and frightening. When she got to the cedar barn glowing eerily in the blackness, she flattened her eye to the wood but then a twig snapped behind her. She swung around to see Earl, a stick of prairie grass between his teeth and he said, Well, well, if it isn't Mary, Mary quite contrary. I see you're a peeping Tom now too.

The girl sways in the darkness carried in a stranger's arms. It is cold, so cold wrapped in the night's black skin. The moon wears a crooked leer. The horizon dissolves into blind naked flesh. Breasts and bums root and flower. A tree of hands offers pleasure and pain. There is the smell of throw-up and the sound of a child crying.

Suddenly she is gliding on a ship. The girl struggles to move and finds only her fingers have life. She attempts to life her head but cannot. Rolling her head to one side she sees she is wearing a white dress and her ship is a coffin.

Faces look down, prayer books in hand, smiling. Someone is dying. A girl with a name she can't remember. Then she is falling. The lid drops with a thud. She is swallowed by fear and darkness.

She surrenders to dying, nostalgic even for the unhappy times. She prays to God to end it all, but there is only silence. She sleeps and dreams she is sleeping.

When she awakens there are three shafts of light, a holy trinity. They fill her heart with hope and she appeals to them with singing. By afternoon the light pools irritate her skin and she turns her face away from them.

Morning. Everyone up and at table. The predictable twitter of the radio, the lingering smell of coffee. Eleanor in housecoat, her hair in rollers, large platinum donuts wrapped in a fire-engine kerchief, a cigarette held between painted fingernails, turning the pages of *Ladies Home Journal.* Even Earl joined them for breakfast, feed cap on backwards, reading the paper with Fergus, who had coffee and Benzedrine, while Sheryl and Josh munched quietly on toast and jam.

Sheryl sat in a haze, wan and thin, a scrape on her cheek, ponytail askew, staring vacantly at the yellow vinyl squares on the tablecloth, saying please and thank you for everything. The world was somehow brand new and beautiful this morning. She felt euphoric and kept touching the plate, the table, her cup, to feel their cold clean solidity. Her thoughts rambled dreamily—maybe her mother would come for her today, Sheryl saw the blue Valiant reversing up the drive until the faces at the table blurred and she felt her thoughts drifting again. There was something she wasn't remembering.

Is it Sunday?

No Tuesday, silly.

You had the flu and ran a high fever, Eleanor explained.

We almost had to call Doc McBrearty but *pencillium notatum*, kiddo, that miracle of modern medicines, did the trick, Fergus said brightly.

Sheryl turned to Josh whose ears were sticking out from his newly-shorn head making him look like a candied apple. He told her they'd taken him to the barber yesterday to get ready for school.

Where's Levon? she asked, and the table abruptly fell silent.

Peter fixed his bicycle, and then he went home.

There was something troubling about this, but she couldn't put her finger on it.

Eleanor said, Eat some cereal.

Sheryl consulted the bunnies in her bowl, but they weren't telling.

Earl read out tidbits from the paper: crop prices and weather, odd scraps of news that interested him.

Lordy, will you get a load of this? Says teener gets two years for sodomy.

Imagine that, Fergus said, pouring himself another cup of coffee.

What's sodomy? Peter asked.

Yeah, Eleanor asked, putting her slippered feet up on Earl's kitchen chair.

That would be, Earl said, when one fella puts his pecker in another fella's behind.

Ouch, Eleanor said.

Peter put down his toast and wiped the corners of his mouth carefully. Sheryl noticed he was pale, and his hand trembled.

I didn't know that was a criminal offense, did you? Earl continued, turning to Fergus matter-of-factly.

First I've heard of it, Fergus said.

A person can go to jail, it seems from this article.

Still there would have to be witnesses, Fergus said. Earl whistled and turned the page, continuing to read quietly. Peter put down his toast.

Eammon knocked on the door and Earl went off with him, Fergus went out onto the porch and Eleanor drifted upstairs. Peter grabbed the newspaper and began rifling through it furiously turning page after page.

That story Earl was talking about. I've looked twice, it's not here. Peter collapsed into his chair and lit himself a cigarette from one of the open packets on the table.

Something was wrong, there was something Sheryl wasn't understanding. She ate her cereal, the painted bunnies appearing beneath the milk in her bowl and then disappearing again when she lifted her spoon. Peter defected to the porch, screen door slamming. The radio nattered ominously about Commies, the Vietnam war. The world was crazy, Sheryl thought.

She got up noiselessly and placed her bowl in the sink, keeping vigil at the kitchen window. She heard Peter talking to Fergus. Peter's voice was high and thin, saying how he didn't like some of what was happening, he was just a kid who wanted to have fun and was only doing what everybody else was doing, and he certainly had never meant to hurt anybody, but Fergus stopped him mid-sentence, putting a large immaculate hand over the boy's mouth.

Fergus told him not to worry. We don't talk about the night in the light of day, kiddo, he said. You don't understand. It's all part of a greater plan. You've got to step out of the old game. You're one of the horsemen now. He gazed off at the yard as though all the mysteries of life were written there. It's an honour to be chosen, he said.

Fergus had his finely buffed fingers around the boy's neck and shook him gently. Sheryl had seen Fergus do that before but couldn't think with who or when. The gesture gave her a sick feeling.

See that animal, what is he? Fergus said, pointing at Lupus, sitting perky-eared against his doghouse. Well, I'll tell you—he's a beast. I've always known, I am THE BEAST. I am HE. He's inside me. Alive. Breathing.

Peter stood squinting into the late summer sun.

He lives inside you too, Fergus chuckled, pointing a bony finger into Peter's chest, adding, One day you'll see that what is good is sometimes bad, and what's bad often brings good. The universe is nothing but a mirror image of your own mind, kiddo. *Pomarium videre non potes propter pomos.* You can't see the orchard for the trees.

Black water, Sheryl whispered, staring into the sink.

That evening Louis Venerable knocked on their door and inquired if anyone had seen Levon, the boy had run away from home again, and Fergus told him no he hadn't been around for over a week. The tall Indian stood there for a long while considering Fergus with his even brown-eyed gaze before accepting this answer and turning to leave. A cool wind rushed into the kitchen from the open door where the family sat silently eating meat loaf. Peter wearing his sunglasses indoors and smoking one cigarette after another. No one had mentioned the flat tire or Levon's bicycle. The radio was on, the horns for the station identification announced the hour, cheerful as always. Dinner was on the table, warm and smelling of tomato sauce.

After dinner Fergus told Sheryl that they would need her help in the orchard until harvest was over. April was feeling poorly and couldn't work regularly, so it had been decided that Sheryl would start school in November. He suggested that a girl of her intelligence and unique gifts might be better served with home schooling. He had stayed home from school during harvest time when a boy himself.

How come Josh gets to go? she whined, struggling to hold back the tears. But Fergus sighed and explained that Josh was just a child and did not have her gifts.

Her uncle said: Remember, Slim, sometimes we have to make sacrifices for others, kiddo.

Sitting on her bed he pulled out a little blue velvet box. Inside was a silver charm bracelet with a rocking horse and a heart and a little dog and the letter M, for Miriam.

You're a good girl, Slim, he said.

He fastened the clasp around her small wrist.

Love me? he asked and she nodded, reluctantly.

Am I not your favourite uncle? and she said yes.

Sheryl squinted up at Mr. Drecker who was pointing toward the firemen combing the shore.

Every year they pull some poor sod out. Fishermen mostly. Ice fishermen too impatient for the season to begin or too stupid to realize it's over.

Fergus nodded and the children huddled together away from the wind, as the sun sank and the sky darkened. Peter stood apart smoking and brooding, wearing Eammon's red plaid flannel jacket, his fingers peeking out from the cuffs, nicotine yellow.

A stray tabby worried Sheryl's ankles, meowing.

So this is a little different it being August and all, Drecker said. I talked to the fellas, he said, pointing to the firemen, and they don't know if he fell in while fishing, at the moment this is just routine, they're leaving no stone unturned ever since that other wee fella went missing. Between you and me and the lamp post, he's probably just a runaway, they almost always turn up sooner or later. Still, they found his fishing rod here and it's possible there's been a mishap, Lord have mercy.

Sheryl introduced her Uncle Fergus to Drecker, the bee man. Fergus nodded, shook the older man's calloused hand.

Ever seen a dead fish? Drecker chuckled. Well, a man doesn't fare any better after a few hours of soaking in lake water, I'll tell you. He regarded the horizon and the raucous blue froth of the lake.

The cat meowed and Sheryl looked down to see Josh tweaking the cat's tail.

Quit it, Josh, she said.

Well, anyway, happens every year I been here.

Yesiree, Fergus said, mimicking the beekeeper's talk.

Course it's a tragedy when it's children. Drecker shook his head sadly. I for one hope we don't find him. The dead are best left to their misery, it's the living cause most of the trouble anyways.

God's truth, Fergus said.

Deaf, I heard.

Couldn't hear a damn thing, pardon my French, Fergus clucked.

He was retarded too, Josh added and Sheryl said, You're the retarded one.

They all watched the firemen milling about the rock, poking at the water. Sheryl turned to scour the hill behind and saw Buzz Drecker's bee truck, parked at the roadside, the bees orbiting the hives in back and she squeezed her elbows tight.

Drecker said, Well, I best be getting back, can't keep the missus waiting forever. Good day to you all then, MacRae, Sheryl-Anne, boys, he nodded and waddled slowly back up the hill.

They stood watching the firemen.

Can we go *now*? Josh whined.

September

Sheryl was awakened Monday night by the piano. She snuck down to the second floor stairwell, stealthy as Nancy Drew, and crouching on the landing she peeked through the oak railing and saw Eleanor splendidly drunk, wearing a slinky sweater suit with animal spots, playing the piano with manicured hands, slamming her fingers onto the keys with a tuneless clamour. Eleanor turned her coiffed head and Sheryl saw that her mascara had run.

You don't love me, do you? Eleanor slurred.

Fergus said nothing, he was reading in the easy chair, legs crossed, scribbling his thoughts in the margins of a book, ignoring her.

You don't even like me, do you? Go on admit it, Eleanor screamed, playing a few noisy bars.

You're drunk, he said finally, quietly, without moving an inch, and Sheryl wished he would say something more to Eleanor, anything, but instead he turned the page with a look of calm disgust, and Sheryl felt sorry for her auntie for the first time.

I'm onto you, Eleanor spat, you're not ruining things again, leaving in the middle of the night in the wake of some scandal. I don't care about all your little friends.

The next morning, Sheryl poured herself a bowl of Cheerios, and Josh made hot chocolate to go with his stack of peanut butter toast, all dressed up for his first day of school, while Fergus and Peter sat smoking and drinking coffee, staring out the window saying nothing at all. Eleanor wore sunglasses and a scarf to breakfast and sat speechless, flipping pages of her *Glamour* magazine with crisp nails. It was so quiet the noises outside the screen door—Lupus barking, a rooster crowing, a combine rumbling down the road—sounded ridiculously loud and Sheryl thought it was funny how they were always pretending everything was normal when it wasn't.

Then out of the blue Fergus started in on Josh.

Who is all that for? he said suddenly, pointing to Josh's leaning tower of toast, and Josh, his neck pinched at the collar from his new checked shirt, stopped buttering to look down at his food, as if surprised to find it there.

Me, sir? he asked sheepishly.

Fergus demanded to know if he had looked in a mirror lately, because if he had he would have seen a fat boy. Fergus launched into a tirade on overeating, pointing out how Josh always took more than his share and reminding him that gluttony was one of the seven deadly sins.

Josh's lower lip began to quiver as he blinked at his plate, and Sheryl whispered under her breath, Don't cry, don't ....

You must establish the right relationship to the universe, kiddo, make yourself a worthy receptacle. To raise yourself to godhead, Fergus stormed, the process is threefold: purification, consecration and initiation, and purification demands abstaining. By overeating you are defiling the temple! From now on you're reducing. I'm not putting up with this nonsense anymore.

No one dared say a word until finally Eleanor gingerly suggested that Josh give Peter some of his toast, and so he slid his plate across the table, tears staining his face. It was a cool September morning but the yellow kitchen was hot and close and even the air seemed unhappy with the radio nattering, the percolator percolating, the cigarette smoke thick and suffocating.

The news came on and the announcer said that a policeman had been cleared of the July shooting of a Negro youngster that had touched off a summer of riots.

Sheryl said: Does that mean it's all over then? But received only blank-eyed stares.

Fergus poured himself a glass of orange juice and, opening up his black medical bag, he toppled pills into his palm for breakfast and downed them one by one with his drink.

In the future we won't need food, he pronounced, we won't eat roughage at all. Did you know that the astronauts have all their food in packets and capsules?

Are those antihistamines? Sheryl asked, and he turned on her with a look that made her wonder why she asked such stupid questions when he was in his picking-on-people mood and she muttered, Sorry, adding, sir, just in case she was in trouble.

We should look to ourselves before we judge others, Fergus corrected her. Sheryl examined her bowl with the carefree bunnies skipping on the sides, having lost all appetite, pondering why adults never followed their own advice.

Fergus hadn't been the same since yesterday afternoon when Louis had come to the door looking for Levon, and Sheryl knew that after dinner Fergus had had words with Earl out on the porch. Then of course there'd been the little talk about school. But even before all that he had eaten almost nothing at dinner and spent hours on the sofa not reading or talking, just lying smoking in the dark like in the bad old days when he was stricken with the sadness and lounged by the blue light of the TV.

What's he doing in there, do you figure? Josh had whispered before bed and Sheryl had shaken her head and shrugged, but privately she thought he was brooding about the end of the world, and she was half afraid that he'd quit his job and pile them all into the Pontiac and whisk them off again somewhere new.

Josh clutched his orange juice with both hands, sniffling and taking little sips, while Sheryl stared at her bowl. Peter slouched, feet up on a chair, his bangs long and drifting into his eyes, greasy and unwashed. One hand traced the outlines of the cheery yellow squares on the tablecloth with his fork until Fergus snapped at him to sit up. Peter shot Fergus a dark look, but adjusted himself, just.

Before he went off to work, Fergus brought out the pictures he'd taken at the beach in July and they all gathered around to humour him, ogling their summer selves in shorts and tans. Arms linked, all smiles, they looked one big happy family, but that time already seemed eons away. Sheryl studied her photographed twin idling with one hand on Josh's shoulder, her dark hair windswept and wild, her face heart-shaped and sunny. She was surprised there was no trace of the nightmares or the voices, perhaps just a slightly strained look about her mouth, otherwise the girl in the picture seemed like a stranger to Sheryl.

After breakfast, she stood in the morning sun with Josh waiting for the school bus, wearing pressed overalls and a clean white blouse with a Peter Pan collar, feeling proud of herself for getting up and ironing her clothes at the crack of dawn, even though she was only going to work in the orchard. Her hair was combed too and parted on the side, tamed by a small blue pony barrette. Eleanor had cut Sheryl's bangs, long flappy bangs that were all the style now and they tickled her eyebrows and she hoped they made her look *assured and humorous and witty* like the magazine said. Most of all she hoped that Peter would notice that she was taking better care of herself.

Swallows and chickadees darted among the oat grass and red-top and horsetail, mocking her with their freedom, while she and Josh knocked about by the roadside, the wind hissing through the tall summer grasses, still secretly miserable and sick with envy that Josh was going to school while she was not. She had graduated beyond her thumbs and bitten her first and second fingers so badly it hurt to wash her hair.

Josh poked at an ant hill with his patent leather shoe and squatted down, plucking the magnifying glass out of his pocket to busy himself frying ants while waiting. Sheryl hummed to herself as Josh's ants struggled silently under the white heat of the glass.

Quit it, she told him, how would you like it if somebody fried you?

Mind your own beeswax, he mumbled.

It's unfair, you get to go and I don't.

It's okay, Slim, he said putting away the magnifying glass. School's not all that great. I'll tell you everything that happens. Promise.

She complained, He picks on me, if my mother were here I could go to any school I wanted. Sheryl tried to conjure the blue Valiant out of the morning mist obscuring the dip in the road.

Yeah, maybe, Josh said, studying the ground. Still, you're his favourite, it's always Slim this and Slim that and he's *my* Dad. You even look like him. Life's unfair, that's all, he shrugged.

The bus crested the rise and descended the hill, a yellow octopus with faces, arms and hands wiggling out its sides. It stopped and devoured Joshua lunch pail and all and belching, the bus motored off leaving Sheryl alone at the roadside.

The Indians appeared in the yard that morning: Louis Venerable, who did all the talking, and his brother Tom, who always wore a hat and a wide grin, his cheeks pockmarked as the surface of the moon. They drove up in an old truck with cardboard for a back window. Tom stood in the yard, arms dangling by his sides, silent and awkward while Louis negotiated for them both. They brought with them good news, Levon Skinner had turned up at the Ernest C. Drury School for the Deaf in Milton, a bit battered but none the worse for wear. He wouldn't talk to anyone or get out of bed for days, but he was on the mend now and back in school, Louis said. His aunt was relieved he was all right and he'd promised her he would never run away again. Finished with shooting the breeze, they put out their cigarettes, picked up their cedar ladders and walked carefully down the tractor road and into the orchard.

Sheryl lounged in bed listening to her transistor. CPAL-AM was replaying a few minutes from a brief concert the Beatles held in Vancouver in August. More than one hundred teenage girls fainted and had to be carried off the Vancouver football field on stretchers. The announcer said there were so many flashbulbs from amateur photographers, it looked as though lightning were striking the bleachers. It was impossible to hear them sing for the endless shrieking. Sheryl had never heard such a sound, it was wild, desperate, deafening. In the end, the Fab Four had played in Canada for only thirty-two minutes. *The Limey kings of beat are taking America by storm*, the announcer raved and Sheryl pictured a world of op art and topless bikinis, concerts and manic teenagers in white kid boots, screaming themselves hoarse, as life changed in ways it never had before, and she felt more trapped and lonely than ever.

The McIntosh were ready early that fall, by the second week of September they were ripe and round and full on the tree. The McIntosh were the sweetest and most popular, their flesh tender and white, not too small or too big, just the right size for fitting in a palm, Fergus always said, equally good for applesauce, apple betty and eating raw.

Come September the orchards were a hive of activity and workers everywhere in the valley picked from dawn until dusk. Mothers, grandmothers, children, crop farmers who'd already harvested, factory workers who'd been laid off, everyone and anyone with two hands was commandeered to help for the six weeks it took to get the Macs in before they dropped off the tree and became grounders good only for canning or apple juice.

Every morning Sheryl was supposed to do her school work, although more often than not she read her Nancy Drews or tried on Eleanor's shoes, drifting about the house bored, her small black radio pressed to her ear, glued to the top forty, dressed ridiculously in shorts and high heels that clicked along the linoleum. But come three o'clock she changed into overalls and rushed out to the orchard to join the others. They worked until dinner time without pause except for half an hour at lunch when they perched on the hay wagon and devoured ham sandwiches Eleanor and April and Sheryl had brought down. The men drank coffee and smoked and talked. Sheryl always tried to squeeze in beside Peter who was growing his hair long now like Bob Dylan so that it hugged his collar and made him look even more like a star.

At the MacRae's the working day began at seven when Louis Venerable appeared in the orchard wearing green rubber boots with his brother Tom in tow, sleepy-eyed and puffing rollies. They always nodded hello to Sheryl but rarely stood around shooting the breeze. The motley crew included the two hired Indians and Eammon and Peter. Tom and Louis worked quietly high up in the twenty-foot trees, while either Peter or Sheryl did the grading and Eammon walked back and forth below barking at them to hurry it up and get their behinds in gear. Then he'd leap up onto the tractor and drive away the full bulk bins, returning with new empties.

They worked long days, sometimes until dark in order to get a block done, their backs sore, their palms stretched and fingers aching, tempers flaring, their heads tired and full of the cawing of startled crows, the stop and start diesel hum of the tractor. Long after they went to bed they could still hear these things and smell the sweet stink of apples lingering on their clothes and skin.

When the day's work was done, the Indians disappeared into the bush and the MacRaes walked up to the main house and collapsed on the porch exhausted, watching the sun fade from orange to purple until it was nothing but a red memory on the horizon, then they shuffled upstairs to bed to begin all over the next morning.

One night Fergus told them the story of the McIntosh. It was after eight-thirty, Josh had already changed into his cowboy pyjamas and lay curled up beside Sheryl in the rocking chair. The evening was thick with cricket song, the nightly bats circling the yard. Fergus informed them that the McIntosh was the most famous apple ever grown in Ontario, discovered by John McIntosh by accident in the early 1800s in Dundas County. He told them how McIntosh came upon the wild apple seedling one day when he was out on a walk. Of all the varieties that grew wild on his farm the McIntosh was the most popular, but try as he might John McIntosh couldn't recreate it, Fergus explained, scratching his constantly itchy nose.

Mother Nature made a fool of John McIntosh for years, Fergus said, until one day a travelling hired man taught him how to attach a bud from the original tree onto the trunk of a new tree and presto! he had his first lesson in grafting, an art perfected by the Greeks thousands of years before.

Fergus lit a Rothmans and continued with his story. The original McIntosh tree lived nearly one hundred years, surviving all manner of Ontario weather, not to mention a fire that burned down the McIntosh farm. The last harvest was picked in 1906 then the tree keeled over from old age, but by then its offspring were all over Ontario.

Oh did I tell you? Fergus added, I heard Levon Skinner turned up at school.

The porch dwellers were silent.

So you see, Fergus concluded cheerfully, everything worked out for the best.

Sheryl and Josh loitered in town, kicking about aimlessly until they could get a ride home with Fergus, window shopping up and down the sun-dappled main street Saturday afternoon, their hands jammed into empty pockets, dodging busy shoppers, browsing storefronts still blaring back-to-school sales.

Sheryl parked herself before Fern's Fashions, glued to the window full of paisley pant-suits and cropped fur jackets, stockings and socks in stripes, lace, diamonds and dots worn with low-heeled white boots with zippers in back. There were even short shimmery T-shirt dresses and a sign: *Should you show your knees? Yes, this year it's legs, legs, legs!!!* And Sheryl felt brave and naked and shivery just looking at them.

When they got bored they slipped into the damp cave of Hindell's Hardware, with its ancient walls covered in tiny cardboard boxes full of screws and nuts and bolts in every size imaginable. They eavesdropped on the farmers huddling about the counter shooting the breeze wearing their caps pushed back on their foreheads, arguing over which was better, the trusty red ensign or that fancy flag with the three maple leafs. They still had another hour to kill so they drifted back outside where the shadows had grown longer and wandered to the edge of town until they saw Harry Madeline scurrying along the street, and they hurried after the bent black man, stopping when he stopped, like spies or thieves, starting when he moved on.

Finally Harry turned into the tiny shingled building that was his home with its patched roof and decaying porch and Sheryl marvelled once again at how Harry's house was not much bigger than their shed at MacRae Brothers' Orchards.

Jeepers Creepers, Josh said, pointing to Harry's stone fence, it's even bigger since the last time we were here. Sheryl nodded.

Have you heard the latest? Mrs. Walcott's Siamese has gone missing, Josh said. Andy and Jeff said the garbage men find little bones in Harry's trash all the time. Jeff figures he stuns the cats with a BB gun and then nabs them. Skins them like rabbits.

Sheryl gasped, horrified.

Either way he's nuts, Josh said, singing: *They're coming to take him away ha!ha! to the funny farm where everything's gay....*

Shshshs.

They waited, hiding behind an old maple down the street as Harry lurched inside. They waited and waited but there was nothing to see, apart from the cats curled in every window, orange and calico and tabby. Harry no longer came in or out. A cloud obscured the sun and Sheryl shivered, the weather had turned as soon as school had started and the evenings were cool now. They made idle conversation to pass the time.

You're sure he's the cat skinner? Sheryl asked.

I'm just repeating what I overheard, Josh said, pulling a small hand-rolled cigarette out of his pocket, saying he'd stolen one of Eammon's faery cigarettes. Should we smoke it? he giggled, grinning mischievously.

No, Sheryl hissed, put that away, we could get arrested. That's what gives Fergus all those harebrained ideas.

Do you think it will really happen? Armageddon and the end of the world and all that stuff in the Bible that he says?

I don't know, maybe, if the Commies drop the bomb, I guess.

Andrew Vanderboch said we'd have about eight seconds to live if they do.

Holy cow, Sheryl said. That's not even enough time to say your prayers.

They practiced saying The Lord's Prayer really fast until they could recite it in under ten seconds.

Eleanor and Fergus do a lot of things that I wouldn't tell anybody but you, Josh confessed, calling his parents by their names, a habit they'd taken to indulging in lately that Sheryl found both thrilling and insolent. She nodded. You know what I don't get? Josh went on. How they go to church every Sunday.

They're not like other people, it's the new game, the new religion for modern times. And anyway, you're not supposed to talk about the night during the day.

Sorry.

You don't get it because of the generation gap, that's all. All the same, don't you grow up to be like them, Sheryl warned.

I won't.

I won't neither, Sheryl said, I'm going to get out of this shit box of a town first chance I get.

Harry's door opened then and the old man slipped out, wearing a long overcoat grey and torn, pockets sagging. He limped down the street, rushing with his odd start and stopping motion, as if he was in a hurry but kept forgetting his destination. The children scurried after him along the road, on a mission, stalking the cat skinner and growing brave in their righteousness. As they followed him they sang, quietly at first: *Mad, mad Madeline gone ahead and lost your mind* … repeating the chant and gradually getting noisier until they were loud and taunting, and Harry spun around and shouted at them to hush their heathen mouths and leave an old man alone, to the grave he was goin'. As Harry slipped into the rhyme his arms flew about in the air and he seemed to battle not with the children but with some phantom there. They turned on their heels and ran up the street as fast as their legs could carry them, giggling and giddy with their own wickedness, until they were out of earshot and stood panting and holding their guilty aching sides.

Sheryl and Peter lay half naked in the dim light of the hayloft sharing a cigarette. Sheryl did up one of the buttons on her shirt and said: Truth or dare?

Truth, he said.

I went to the summer place, to bring back the kittens before it gets cold. Still no National Velvet, she told him.

Peter nodded and zipped up the trousers of his blue coveralls, leaving the shirt open.

Your turn.

Truth for me too.

I've been working on "The House of the Rising Sun." I'll play it at the next hootenanny soon as I get all the chords down, but my fingers are all cramped up. I don't think this apple picking is any good for playing guitar. Your Uncle Fergus has said I can go to Yorkville and stay with his friends after the harvest, first I have to put my repertoire together, but Jesus, there's never any time to practice anymore.

Sheryl nodded and told him that orchard life was hard. In the old days when Fergus was studying and they lived in Toronto all they did was watch TV after school and eat peanut butter toast. Here it was work, work, work, and in the fall it got worse. Even she was busy with grading and feeding all the animals. They could hear Lupus barking outside at a truck escaping down the road.

I don't know what makes him so crazy, she said. Josh says Lupus has got maggots, it's just too gross. I guess he needs a bath, but who can get near him? His sores never get any better because he's always dragging his bum through the dirt. Afterwards he licks them clean, but before you know it a car comes by and he's up and running and the whole thing starts all over.

Peter nodded, stupid mutt, and went back to griping. I don't care if I see another apple ever again. Man, that smell is all over me, it's under my fingernails.

Yeah, Sheryl nodded. It's a drag being tired all the time.

Truth or dare?

Forget it, I don't feel like playing anymore.

I dare you to go all the way with me, here, right now, she said, staring up at the barn roof, exhaling. No one would ever know.

Sheryl, are you trying to get me arrested? We've gone far enough. If Eammon caught me up here with you he'd kill me.

Sheryl got up and looked out the little octagonal window. The wind stirred the row of cedars by the house. A red squirrel burrowed among the withering pansies, stashing nuts. Outside the sky was mauve and Sheryl noticed with a queasy flutter that the sun was already sinking, the days shrinking as they headed into autumn.

Peter still lay smoking. His face looked weary in the dim light. It's already getting dark, Sheryl said. In fall the nights are so long.

Mirror, mirror on the wall, who's the fairest of them all? Earl joked and the men dissolved in laughter.

Fergus and Eammon, Peter and Earl were sitting around the table smoking their funny cigarettes, laughing and talking and occasionally tottering off to the bathroom together in groups like little girls, returning wiping their noses and giggling. Fergus had one of Eleanor's hand mirrors and carried it around with him everywhere.

What's the mirror for? Sheryl asked them, but they just laughed at her.

Horse for the horsemen, Fergus joked mysteriously.

The men had taken to playing poker Friday evenings, sitting around the kitchen table bluffing and drinking Red Cap beer. April didn't attend because she was still under the weather so Eleanor didn't either, opting instead to watch television with Josh in the other room.

Tonight Sheryl could tell the men were up to something, they snickered like children. Sheryl brought them their beers, *snappa cappa red cap*, and they let her hang around for a bit. She plunked herself down on a small stool, nervously listening to them talk, her eyes stinging from the smoke in the kitchen and the stench of burnt lawn, the photograph of the summer family smiling down on them.

Lately Fergus had started wearing his smoking jacket to dinner and Sheryl was convinced the shiny blue coat changed his personality. He became demanding and imperious, ordering Sheryl and Eleanor around. Get me the ashtray on the counter, will you? he would ask Sheryl when it was closer to him than to her, acting as though he were an English gentleman on loan. He wore his Highland tam tonight with the satin jacket, and Sheryl couldn't decide whether this get up made him look mod or just truly bizarre.

He interrupted the hilarity and card-playing for a thoughtful moment. He slid his glasses up his nose and said, Did you know young Peter that you could save the world's forests, wouldn't have to cut down a tree, could start a whole new industry if we only grew hemp, marijuana as a cash crop? The whole world could be transformed so simply by a little cultivation of *cannabis lativa*. No fertilizers necessary, no pesticides, the T.H.C. in every plant is enough to turn the nose of every bug worth calling an insect. The day will come, kiddo, you'll see, when we grow hemp for paper, for fuel, for clothing even. The possibilities are endless but it's change people fear.

Amen to that, Earl said, and Eammon echoed him.

Everyone regarded Fergus with awed silence as he handed Peter the reefer. Peter sucked on it and held his breath, his cheeks two red balloons that exploded in coughing, and Sheryl wondered why they all held their breath like that when all it did was make them choke.

Peter coughed and coughed and all four started laughing until they cried, although Sheryl didn't see the joke.

My, my, doesn't Mary here look more like her mother every day, Earl winked. Sheryl flushed red.

Peter said, No man, she looks like Fergus, but Eammon pointed out he had never met Miriam.

Am I like her? she asked Fergus.

He nodded slowly and said, Just a wee bit, Slim.

Fergus clapped his hands. I've finally decided on the next step for our young protege here. A way for him to prove himself on the secret path, Fergus said, eying Peter warily. It can't be all fun and games, after all. The disciple must test his mettle. I have my eye on a new contraption, a Honeywell Elmo Pocket Auto Zoom 83, an 8-millimetre movie camera that works on batteries for the man at home. Horsemen, I propose we make a movie. I'm ready to experiment with moving pictures and you, Angelboy—our handsome baby face, Cedar Hollow's own Jimmy Dean—I think you should be the star, our very own screen legend. What do you think of that, kiddo?

Peter's face brightened, and he ran a hand through his dirty-blond hair, his dimple deepening.

Fergus went on: It will be both myth and ritual. Artaud's *Theatre of Cruelty* with a little Brecht thrown in. Larger than life, a retelling of the greatest story of all, a biblical tale, the Osiris legend, divine and profane, shedding light on mysteries centuries old. And best of all, my movie will make Peter Angelo here famous. He can put it on his resume. Maybe we'll even have screenings, he said. Am I brilliant?

Everyone agreed he had outdone himself.

A movie—holy smokes! Peter said, sitting up in his chair. He snapped his fingers. You—you're amazing, you always know just the thing. I love the movies, man. Far out! I'm game, if everyone else is. He was grinning from ear to ear.

Can I have a part? Sheryl asked, and Fergus adjusted his glasses, saying, Yes, yes of course, a part for Slim, a part for everyone. Fabulous, it's all settled then.

He added one more thing. He told them they would shoot in October after the Spys, the final October apples were all in and volunteered Eammon and Peter to fix up the old barn with a wood stove so that they could shoot inside somewhere warm.

Sheryl thought of nights black as coal, daylight diminishing, the cold north wind rattling the old house.

We'll make our movie at the time of year when darkness is equal to light and the veil between the two worlds is thinnest, Fergus said, staring into his drink as though the secret of life were hidden there.

It happened soon after. Summer came to a close. Sheryl smelled a premonition of frost in the dawn air. There was a paleness in the yellow sun-worn grass and a chill lingered in the cedars as the shadows lengthened at the end of the day.

It rained for an entire week. The geese squawked overhead in ragged formation heading south as hunting season opened and there was the crackle of occasional gunfire. On the brisk walk out to the barn to feed Lupus in the mornings, the maples sprouted out of the mysterious morning fog, their edges orange. As Sheryl stumbled around the corner of the barn towards Lupus's circle she found him sitting beside his bowl watching her with those intense blue eyes, waiting for his breakfast.

While Eleanor was getting ready for her Avon appointments in the morning, Sheryl quickly read through her homework. She had learned the names of the Great Lakes, finished *Romeo and Juliet*, had read through the War of 1812. Regardless, as soon as Eleanor's heels clattered out the door, Sheryl pulled out her Nancy Drew. She'd finished *The Secret of Red Gate Farm*, and was onto *The Bungalow Mystery*.

Laura blinked her eyes, then said soberly, "You don't understand. You see my mother passed away a month ago and- " She could not continue.

Nancy impulsively put an arm around Laura's shoulders. "I do understand," she said, and told of losing her own mother at the age of three.

Three. The last year Sheryl had spent living with her own mother, the coincidence endeared her even more to Nancy.

Bored, she stole into Eleanor's bathroom. In one of her auntie's magazines, Sheryl found an article that declared: 1964--*The Year that Youth Took Over All Paris! Anybody in Europe over twenty-five might as well drop dead!* There were pictures of peaceniks from the ban-the-bomb movement and ads for Moon Drops bath oil and Dep styling gel, all modelled by razor-thin girls with swinging hair, fluttering doe eyes and lips pale and skin-coloured. Sheryl knew no one who looked like that in Eden Valley.

She put back the magazine and tried on her auntie's frosted lipstick and backless leopard pant-suit, struggling with the gluey Eye-lusion eyelashes. Then stood batting her huge eyes in the mirror at herself.

One night it rained and rained and the shutters slammed from the tantrum wind and ragged leaves scurried across the yard. When the men came up to the house they were soaking wet, and Fergus seemed agitated. He wiped his nose constantly and paced the kitchen, passing on the minute steak Eleanor had warmed up for him, while outside Lupus started his crazy barking, a series of roars and high-pitched strangling yelps as though roused by the spirit of the storm.

Peter was drunk and moody and griped, What is wrong with that dog, man? Why doesn't someone put him out of his goddamn misery?

The whole table turned to look at Fergus. Sheryl filled the silence. Lupus hates trucks, he was hit by a truck. He probably heard one out on the road.

Fergus stood up suddenly, his eyes huge and startling behind his boxy glasses. It's time I took care of things, he said and hustled Josh outside, who argued, Jeepers creepers, why me? Why do I have to go?

Sheryl watched them from the kitchen window, washing dishes, while they trundled out to the shed, Eleanor tidying up after dinner, pitter-pattering about the kitchen in fluffy angora slippers that made her look as if she was wearing kittens on her feet. Lupus was a deranged white sentinel in the darkness, still madly barking, the rain spitting down, the yard brown and drizzled, the incessant drip, drip from the eavestrough.

Fergus and Josh emerged from the shed with a baseball bat, Josh stumbling over his own feet, and when they got to Lupus, Fergus began shouting, his crow's hair slathered to his head in the September rain. Sheryl saw that her cousin's freckled face was red and puffy from crying. Fergus began swinging at the dirty white crippled dog while Lupus spat and snarled, and Sheryl slunk down against the kitchen cupboards, until her thin body settled on the black and white tiled floor, her face in her hands.

When the sun rose the next morning the valley was silvery and dew-covered. Sheryl put on her yellow raincoat and went out into the yard to check on Lupus. His black nose poked out of his dog house for a moment to sniff the air, but he didn't growl or bark or attempt to come out to defend his little piece of yard and she felt sorry for him, no one liked him because he was ugly and crippled and made too much noise. Feeling reckless, she inched forward until she was standing just a few feet from him and told him all this, talking out loud to him in a cooing gentle voice like you would a baby. She heaped his bowl with food and dropped it not a foot from his house, pushing the clay bowl forward with the toe of her rubber boot but there was nothing, not a whimper. Still she could feel him huddled inside there wild, watchful, distrusting her. She did something daring then. She picked up a pork chop from the bowl and tossed it into the dark mouth of his house and heard his jaws clamp around the bone, catching it expertly in mid-air, and she felt there was an unspoken truce between them. She said, Good dog, and heard him pause in his crunching to listen to her voice.

The rain made picking that day miserable, the Indians wore plastic garbage bags under their baseball caps and raincoats and worked oblivious of the weather, but Peter didn't know these tricks and every time he lifted his head his hood fell off and the rain dripped down his back. Sheryl's new bangs were plastered against her forehead, her skin felt damp inside her macintosh, her toes cold, her fingers wrinkled and raw. They worked quietly in the rain, silenced by the hissing all around them.

At five, the Indians disappeared back into the bush, following a short cut by the river to their shabby weatherworn house, and Sheryl and Peter slowly walked up to the barn, Sheryl's arms heavy from working all afternoon. Mercifully the rain stopped, and the sky was gradually clearing, so she talked Peter into taking a bit of a detour. They zigzagged through the trees to the back of the MacRae property, until they reached a block in the lee of a hill, safe from the frost and with an auspicious southeastern exposure, where Eammon grew a cluster of heirloom varieties. Sheryl knew of Eden Block but had rarely been there.

Eammon says that to pay the bills they have to grow the apples that sell, that will last a lifetime on the shelf. Supermarket apples, Sheryl told Peter, hands on her hips. They grow them in orderly rows on midget trees so they're easy to pick, so they look the same and ripen all at the same time, then pack them onto a truck and bump them along, shipping them all the way to hell's half-acre and back. We grow the kind of apples that will sleep nicely in cold storage through the winter months, but in the end a sleeping beauty is never as tasty as an apple fresh from a tree.

Peter shook off his hood. The sun struggled to break through cloud and when it did the light was sharp and rainwashed, blinding.

The really beautiful apples, the ones that taste like heaven, these we keep for ourselves, she grinned. In his private block Eammon grew fifty varieties with bizarre fancy names like Beverly Hills and Ellison Orange, Hollow Log and Ladies Finger. Apples that tasted like bananas, pears, cantaloupes, lilacs and almonds; some that smelled like cinnamon and roses and Kool-Aid even. Sheryl's rubber boots cut large swathes through the uncut twitch grass as she showed Peter how Eammon grew many cultivars on one tree, a different apple on every branch. Producing a pocket knife she cut Peter slices of fruit, and they grazed from tree to tree, comparing each new taste, the wind high in the branches, soaring heavenward.

The next day at noon the screen door slammed and Eammon came in, hair tossed, face red, grumbling that it was nasty outside, roads flooded. He poured himself a cup of coffee and told them all that Harry Madeline had died. Some railway workers had found him on the tracks.

They think he was out wandering, gathering those stones of his, and he got disoriented and was hit by a train, Eammon said. There was some talk of foul play, but the police chief ruled that out. Eammon said he had heard over at Hillman's Hardware.

Jeepers, Josh whispered, Slim, we were probably the last people to see him alive.

After lunch Saturday Sheryl and Josh cycled the CCM into town, the air smelling of burning wood from fireplaces newly stoked. Geese struggling into formation overhead.

When they got there the little house was quiet and the chimney smokeless, the stone piles were still in the yard and several tatty collarless cats sat on the sinking porch, meowing with scratchy, battle-weary voices. Feeling brave, Josh rattled the knob and found the door was unlocked and when no one was looking they slipped inside, the cats with them. There was hardly any furniture, just a little kitchen table and a chair, a chipped cup and a package of Nescafe, a stained mattress on the floor, the walls dirty and painted turquoise, the smell of cat pee everywhere. Their footsteps echoed empty and hollow. They explored the house, daring to open one door after another until they found a room full of rocks piled high as the light fixture.

Crikey, Josh said. Madeline was totally certifiable.

They stood for a moment in awe before the mound of rubble, which seemed as senseless to Sheryl as Harry's demise.

Eammon told me they think the cats will stop disappearing now. People blamed him for Ralph McDonald too.

Josh stared wide-eyed. Then, inexplicably, he started to sniffle.

What's wrong? Sheryl asked, surprised.

He covered his face with his mittens and began to cry.

What tell me! She insisted, shouting at him.

I did it, he blubbered, finally. I'm sorry. I cut up the kittens. I didn't mean to, it just happened. Don't tell anyone, promise … but he couldn't finish his sentence because Sheryl slapped him hard.

After church on Sunday Sheryl sat in the passenger seat of the Pontiac while Fergus bent over the steering wheel in the grip of that peevish roaming. He had dropped Eleanor and Josh off at the house and insisted Sheryl come for a drive, and they travelled erratically now from town to town drifting further away from Cedar Hollow until they were on a nameless sidestreet in a small middle-class neighbourhood. Fergus slowed the Bonneville and pulled alongside a small playground to watch a little girl skipping rope. Sheryl stared dumbfounded as she registered the face of the girl, so like her own, the dark hair, a small scar on her cheek, the grey eyes. She was like a younger sister to Sheryl.

Give her this licorice, Fergus said, and ask her if she knows where the carnival is. Go on, Mary, get out.

No, Sheryl said, clenching her teeth. No, I won't.

The projector flickered in the dark of the living room, the smoke a dervish in its beam. In the movie Peter was dressed up in one of Fergus's clean pressed shirts, Brylcreem slicked through his longish hair, a bandana slung around his neck. He sang and played guitar on camera but he was sloshed and kept screwing up chords or slurring his words. He couldn't get through one whole song and always had to start over again. Way to go, Earl shouted out of the darkness and Sheryl could hear the disapproving groan of Fergus's eggplant easy-chair.

The girl dreams of a circle upon a circle: a circle of light from a bare bulb, the moon's circle face, a chalk circle on the floor. Bodies sway by a wood stove within a nimbus of pale light. Water boils.

In the center of the circle a woman, naked, her belly round and white as a full moon. The woman groans and struggles. There is blood in the triangle between her legs. Candles glow around her. The woman cries, and a small creature comes into the world. It has a huge, ugly head, and the body of a small crab. It makes a mewling sound, mouth puckering in little fish kisses.

The half-dressed bodies gather round.

Give me my baby! the woman shrieks.

The girl looks on while the small creature is silenced.

Death sucks all air from the room and it is quiet for a moment, mouths open and close, but the girl cannot hear them.

Sheryl lay on her back on the old flat stone in the summer place, staring up at the sky through her binoculars, turning clouds into Corvettes and horses, rabbits and dogs. After awhile she heard footsteps and watched as Peter struggled up the hill, his face swollen, purple circles under his eyes. The rain had stopped, but it was damp and chilly, and he wore a plaid lumber jacket against the cold and blew on his hands to warm them. The first two fingers were nicotine-stained, the fingernails yellow as an old man's.

Hey there, he called nervous, jittery. What are you doing up here all by yourself on a Sunday morning, Slim?

Nothing, Sheryl said, stuffing the binoculars inside her jacket pocket. What are you doing down there?

Not much, he said and kicked at a clump of dirt that dislodged and rolled down the hill gathering wet grass. There was a wind, it often rode up the middle of the valley off the lake, caught in the bowl between the escarpment and the water and whirled in circles, chasing its own tail.

Not hungry, I guess, eh? he asked.

Nah, she said. She could hear the water from the small creek all of a sudden. It was always doing that, getting loud out of the blue, as though talking in a thin, cold voice.

Can you hear it? she asked him. The trees along the escarpment were just starting to turn, the valley was most beautiful in fall, the maples speckled yellow and orange, the leaves dried and brittle. She could feel nature all around her on the verge of withering into autumn.

He squatted down with his back to the boulder and pulled out his cigarette pack.

It always sounds like the water's saying something, she said.

Course, I believe anything could happen here. He took a carefully rolled reefer out of his cigarette pack and lit it up, standing up to offer her some but she declined.

I guess I'm never gonna be Pat Boone, Slim. I just want to have a good time, you know? I think of my mother cooking and cleaning every day, and my old man out every Saturday night drinking beer with his buddies and coming home to smack her around. The world is unfair, man. It's her birthday today.

Sorry, you must miss her. Are you going to call home?

Nah. Anyway, that's not what I came up to tell you. There's trouble down at the farm. Fergus and Earl are both over at Eammon's place right now. I think I did something stupid—I let slip on Thursday that Levon was at the farm on the night he ran away. I told Louis that I fixed his bicycle. I don't know, somehow it just came out, he was asking, fishing around, I think Levon must have said something and that's why the Indians didn't show up Friday.

Oh, Sheryl said, confused.

They were paid last week. If they don't come back, man, I'm gonna go insane. You know how many apples there are still to pick?

Sheryl said, Don't worry, they'll come back.

He shook his head, looking despondent. They both watched the wind tossing a clutch of thin feathery leaves about the hard ground.

Sometimes it feels like I'm stuck in sleep. I want to wake up, but I can't. I feel like I'm awake in my dreams and asleep in real life. I'm not sure I know who I am. She stared up at the troubled sky.

I don't know half what goes through your head, Slim, he chuckled and took another toke. It was probably just a bad dream.

There's always a girl in my dreams who looks like me but isn't me, she said. Once I dreamt Lupus went totally insane and came after me.

Fucking Lupus, man, Peter said. You're having the dreams, 'cause Lupus is barking half the night, and it's getting on your nerves. He looked at the joint, rolling it over and over between his stained fingers. He coughed once or twice, a smoker's hack. He coughed all the time now she realized.

Maybe, Sheryl shrugged. I dreamt about a baby too. A baby was born and then he was … he died. It was horrible. There were people there but I couldn't see their faces. I'm afraid to sleep, she said, I'm afraid to eat.

Peter stopped toking and stood squinting up at her. The joint accidentally burned his fingers and he dropped it in the damp grass. Shit, he said, rifling through bits of furry mullein trying to retrieve it, but no luck. Shit, fuck, he swore again, I really needed that joint, man. Figures my last one, damn, this is not my day. He looked up at her, back at his hands, then he stuck them in his pockets as though to keep them out of trouble.

You're not supposed to talk about the night during the day, he said.

I think you were in the dream, Sheryl said, but it sounded like a question. Then she added: Maybe because I know you now you're in the dreams too.

He looked down at his shoes, tapping them together, nervously. He was wearing a pair of Eammon's old sneakers with different coloured laces and they were wet through. As he bent his head to look at his toes, his long hair shook forward and Sheryl thought he looked like a hobo, like the guys who ride the trains and never settle down or take a job, with his yellow fingers and mittenless hands, his thin coat. He was still beautiful when he smiled, and she thought he would always be beautiful, no matter what.

That was no dream, Slim, he said faintly, almost in a whisper, his head cocked sideways peering at her, something in his eyes. She felt sick to her stomach, the wind suddenly bitter, the tinkling of the stream cruel and hollow.

Was too, she said, sulkily.

He shook his head and glared at her, angry now for some reason. I was there, man, I saw it all. The candles and the manger and that. We're not supposed to talk about it. It's just a game. I was so high for all I know, the abortion wasn't even real.

She was shaking her head, frowning, the clouds threatening worse weather. They could hear Lupus barking. Peter Angelo danced a little from side to side, fidgeting and nervous, trying to keep warm.

I don't remember, Sheryl said.

Man, I can hardly remember I was so wasted. It was Fergus, Peter said, he's the one who started the hootenannies and the secret rites, the new world and the dress-up and everything. It's a big game. Life's a game, he chuckled, but his voice was thin and unhappy.

You know the new religion and the two gods, the preparation for Armageddon. You have to be willing to do stuff to usher in The Change. Things just got out of hand, he said, that's all. His voice was a strained whisper, oddly imploring. She thought he was on the verge of crying.

I mean it probably wouldn't have lived anyhow, it was too young, and April couldn't deliver, I don't know they said she had some weird complication. For all I know the baby wasn't even real.

April? Sheryl asked.

Give me my baby! the woman shrieks.

Peter lit a cigarette. Look Sheryl, let's forget about it, I don't want to talk about this, talking about this stuff doesn't make me feel so good, I promised...anyway it's too late now. He hung his head.

Sheryl stood squinting at the valley below. The ground was yellow and brown in places, soiled; the sky livid and thick with weather. Sheryl got down from her boulder.

No, it was a dream, I would have remembered....

You were there, Slim, Peter said, but she put her hands over her ears and turned away, walking down the hill.

I was not, she yelled back at him.

You were too, Sheryl-Anne, he yelled down at her, losing control. Don't think you're better than us, you weren't dreaming. You're just pretending to yourself. You've been pretending to yourself all along. You were there and you went along with it, just like everybody else.

Sheryl turned and shrieked: You're a liar! I woke up and I was in my bed. And with that she tore off down the hill.

Sheryl thundered through the forest. Plants, earth, trees, reached out for her. The earth tripped her and she stumbled. The sky somersaulted and she lay on her back in the mud. Nothing was certain anymore, no one could be trusted. The wind, the gentle rustling of the stream, these familiar things had been hiding a secret. She scrambled to her feet, they possessed the key to a mystery she did not want to know and the only thing she does know is that somehow she has been betrayed but she's not sure why, by whom, and for how long.

Sheryl streaked through the yard, slammed the front door and clattered up the stairs to her room where she barricaded the door with the little white dresser, heedless of the wood scraping across the hardwood floor, Eleanor outside demanding, What is going on? But Sheryl doesn't know what's wrong. She dragged her desk over, her black hair a flurry, face flushed, and all the photographs of her beloved Northern Dancer, that bay four-legged phenomenon fifteen hands high, fluttered to the floor.

Quickly she piled on as many clothes as she could, because she was so cold. She heard barking. Bark, bark, bark went the mad dog. They were all outside the room knocking on the door. She wrapped the chenille coverlet around her head and sat rocking, her hands over her ears to keep the dreadful noise out, but to no avail, because the dog's crazy bark was in the room, the buzzing of the bees too. Her head was full of voices chastising her: *You're a selfish, blackhearted girl just like your mother, we should have sent you to the Children's Aid, You best forget about your mother, she won't be coming back for you now....* And Sheryl screamed: Shutupshutupshutup I'm not listening. The girl was in the room with all her bloody dreams, and Sheryl put on the record player loud to drown out the noise *She Loves You, yeah, yeah, until the bed shakes and the man is there, deep in the belly of the night, jiggling her shoulder, his eyes red and wide and his breath smelly.*

She is three years old, and it's her birthday, and the man says: Don't you want to see the horsy? They hold hands and tiptoe through the dew in the grass, following the light from a kerosene lantern. Inside the barn, naked people blink in the candlelight. Eponey is there, restless and snorting, shifting from hoof to hoof.

The man puts a needle into the mare's neck, saying she is sick and needs some medicine. Eponey sways, then stumbles over like a woozy drunk in the hay, whinnying. She tries to get up but her legs buckle. The girl starts to cry. As the mare lies there snorting, an older man helps the tall man tie the mare's neck to the stall. He ties her two front hooves together and then her two back hooves, pulling them as far apart as they will go and fastening them with rope to stall posts. The mare whinnies.

The tall man kneels by the horse and calls to the girl: Come here, honey. Come see the horsey.

The barn suddenly seems big and cold and smelly in the candlelight. The girl goes over and sits by the mare's belly in the hay. She pats the horse's wet flank saying, Hello pony.

The girl doesn't see the hand. Doesn't see the knife.

The man bends over the horse and thrusts. The mare bellows, her big head flying back, nostrils flaring; she struggles, her eyes rolling. The second man leans on her neck, while the tall man continues cutting straight down Eponey's belly, which is not a belly at all anymore but a bloody, gaping mouth. The mare continues her chilling scream, while the man buries his hands in her.

The girl screams too, until a warm wet hand grasps her by the neck and she is forced head first into the horse.

Darkest night descends. Blood oozes into the girl's mouth, her ears, her eyes. Screaming soundless in an airless tunnel, she kicks and struggles and smashes at the horrible mass of flesh that drowns her, but her kicking harms the horse, oh beautiful horse! and makes the mare struggle harder; the two held fast together in their terror and misery by one hand--a hand which holds the girl by the throat and prevents her from bursting out as she punches and kicks towards the crack of light...

When she can see again, her Uncle Fergus is there holding her, while she swings wildly at him, swiping the glasses off his head, the window open letting in a cold breeze. He repeats over and over: Calm down, Slim, calm down, it's okay, rocking her back and forth until the room stops sizzling and the voices quiet. When Sheryl is too tired to cry anymore he gives her a pill to take and some milk to drink, something to make her sleep, to take the bad feelings away and she gazes up at him confused, grateful. He cradles her in his arms rocking, saying over and over, That's my girl, you were just dreaming, Slim, your mother was the same, it's just a dream, a bad, bad dream.

The next day, when Peter came up to the house for lunch Sheryl ambushed him on the stairs and told him she had gotten a letter from her mother and he had to take her there, she had the address and phone number and some money, enough to get him started in Toronto. She had found the spare keys to Eammon's truck. When he stalled and asked why couldn't they wait a while she told him that she'd confessed to her Uncle Fergus what Peter had said the other day. There was no time. He blanched. They stole Eammon's truck that afternoon while everyone was out. She walking slowly, sleepwalking to greet it, carrying her small pink valise, Fergus's stash of money an anvil in her pocket ridiculously heavy and incriminating.

Get in, Peter said, stony-faced.

She stared out at the dirty leaf-strewn streets as they drove, silent as a funeral procession, not talking. They were running away finally, and it should have been a happy time but she didn't feel happy, the mood inside the cab was dismal as the weather outside. She turned to him once, smiling and said: Truth or dare? just to cheer him up, but he didn't smile. Instead, he said they'd already dared enough and he didn't want to know any more truths. With that he turned on the radio, lit a cigarette and offered her one. She told herself that everything would work out grand, they'd have an apartment and she'd get a job at Woolworth's and find her mother. She calmed herself with all the happily-ever-after stories she could possibly dream up.

How much money did you get? he asked her after a while, and she showed him, counting out $400 cash. He whistled and said he had as much, no more, in his bank account, Fergus had been saving his wages for him, still every time he'd asked for some money Fergus had given him only cigarettes and a twenty here and there.

A fella can't be blamed for wanting his own money, can he? he asked weakly, as though frightened of the answer.

They drove for an hour, hurtling through a September rain that swamped the windshield wipers. The excitement quickly wore off, replaced by the worried glare of headlights from the other cars and the sad, squishy rhythm of the wipers. Sheryl dozed on and off and awakened with her head cold and flat against the window. It had gotten dark so fast. In fall the darkness was total, the night cold and unforgiving. It was only just supper time. They stopped in at a trucker's rest stop and had dinner, chicken a la king with mashed potatoes and gravy and black forest cake still half-frozen. There was a little variety store next door, and they loitered there, unsure of how to spend their money or their time, buying magazines and chewing gum and Cokes. Outside Peter asked her to show him the address of her mother's house. When she stood staring down at her shoes, he hit the side of the phone booth with his bare hand. Damn, he said, I knew it. You don't know where the hell you're going. Man, why did I let myself get talked into this?

It was now getting late, and the rain was still coming down hard. There was a motel next door, the neon sign blinking in the darkness. Confused about where to go, they decided there was no hurry, they might as well head on out in the morning, so they booked a room as sister and brother. As ridiculous as it was no one questioned them.

Peter sat on one of the twin beds drinking a bottle of Scotch he'd snitched from Fergus's liquor cabinet and smoking a joint. There was carpeting but no TV and every once in a while lights travelled the wall from cars passing on the highway outside. The fluorescent lights turned their skin green, and the door was wooden and the room was damp and smelled of ammonia and moth balls. Sheryl said she would like to go to bed now and got undressed in the bathroom and came out and perched in her nightie on the edge of the bed in the fluorescent glare. She told him she felt like a newlywed. Peter smirked, a little tipsy. She said they were alone now and no one would know they might as well. She felt she owed him something, after all the trouble she caused him. And to her surprise he came over and lay with her and she lifted up her nightie and he took off his jeans and she closed her eyes, counting to herself, 1 2 3 4 5 6, feeling lost and alone, knowing he felt afraid too, even though they were miles away from MacRae Orchards.

Afterwards Sheryl would remember the rush of cars out on the wet road, the lights flashing across the ceiling, the lonely sounds of the highway outside their door.

Sheryl bit her tongue and held him. It hurt and he said he was sorry; she thought it would be different with him, but it wasn't, still she told him to keep going. And when the pain was at its worst a funny thing happened. She began to rise until she was on the ferris wheel with her mother. She remembered the last time Mimi had come to visit before she disappeared for good when Sheryl was four. Sheryl was at the CNE holding a giant pink candy floss, the air was full of carnival song. Miriam talked the conductor into letting Sheryl go on the ride and the troublesome world listed small and toy-like far below. They wheeled round and round together, laughing, the ferris wheel gently rising and falling, and she was happy and light, vaguely aware of her naked prone body on the motel bed. And Sheryl knew then that that's all she had ever wanted, not Peter, not to run away, not Toronto, just for her mommy to come and take her home. And she started to cry then and suddenly the ferris wheel was gone and she was her old wretched self again and Peter was out of control, saying: Oh, oh, oh my. He pulled himself out and spilt all wet and sticky hot over her thigh.

It was all over in a minute.

Are you all right, Slim? he asked and she nodded, her mouth twisting with the effort of trying not to cry. When she didn't answer his voice grew tremulous, worried.

Girls never like it the first time, he said. She didn't tell him it wasn't her first. Instead, she limped into the little tiled washroom and crouched in the tub to clean herself, but no blood appeared. And when she looked up at the bathroom tiles for a moment she thought she saw the numbers 11:11 written there, and she knew that no matter how far she ran she would never escape the pictures inside her head, she could no longer pretend or forget, they would follow her wherever she went.

They lay together in one of the twin beds in the dark afterwards, the neon sign of the motel blinking off and on and reflecting on the sad walls. They each had a cigarette, and Peter said to her, Your mother never did write to you, did she, Slim? She never did plan to come back for you, did she?

Sheryl confessed that she'd made all that up and said she was sorry for lying but it had felt real she'd wished those things for so long. She also wasn't sorry because she'd gotten to run away with him just like she'd always wanted, and they had been together even if she hadn't liked it as much as she'd hoped. She asked him if she was his girl now, and he said he guessed so and he let her lie with her head on his shoulder for a long while and that was the best part, lying there together until they fell asleep.

In the morning when there was a knock on the door they weren't surprised to see Fergus standing there.

October

Sheryl lies spread-eagled in the flatbed of Eammon's truck, dozing, clouds hustling overhead, hair falling across her cheek, surrendering to sleep and waking, again and again, until that horse, that beautiful Appaloosa mare nuzzles her hand, the grey mare's hot breath and velvet muzzle snooping for apples in her open palm. Eponey whinnies in that tender horsy way of hers, waking the girl, but when Sheryl opens her eyes and sits up, there is nothing there. Just the hurtling clouds and October sky. An arrow of geese overhead. The smell of damp earth, the persistent autumn mist creeping along the ground clinging to gullies and tree roots, rendering the world filmy and obscure.

It is All Hallow's Eve and although the wind is chill, there have been a few days of feeble sunshine, the last gasp of Indian summer. In the final week of September a big wind had come up and a third of the McIntosh crop was lost. Sheryl thought of Levon Skinner as she listened to the apples fall all night long, plop, plop, plop. Minus Louis and his men there was no help for it. The others worked past dark, Fergus rigging up his huge photography lights for them, to harvest the last of the apples—the Northern Spies. As the weather grew cool they worked around the clock, wearing windbreakers and bulky sweaters, fingers burning and legs numb, the yard a chaos of picking pails, cedar ladders, bulk bins and brimming orchard boxes. But finally the apples were all in and the whole season was not lost.

The funeral for Harry Madeline wasn't well attended. Sheryl had cycled into town alone, watching the proceedings from the seat of the CCM. Eammon said all Harry's people were gone or had moved away. No more cats had gone missing. No one gossiped about Harry anymore. They said how he was kind, had taken in strays, and given children candy while he lived off a poor man's diet of squirrels, which he shot from his back porch.

Sheryl lies in Eammon's truck now too tired to move, staring upwards. The songbirds have all escaped south. The sky is silent and white and restful but for the occasional gun shot. The maples are on fire, the oaks the colour of pumpkins, the leaves a sweetly fermenting carpet. The storefronts in town are decorated in black and orange, with coloured-paper cut-outs of goblins and jack-o-lanterns, ghosts, witches, bats and cats that Sheryl finds silly and ominous all at once. In places where the rain and wind have been fierce the tree limbs are bare, mere X-rays of themselves.

It is dark every day by six now, dark when she rises and dark when they finish picking, and daylight feels like a brief reprieve in a sandwich of perpetual night. It is Sunday night forever now. Her heart is sombre too, then she remembers: They are making The Movie. A gun goes off and Sheryl jolts upright.

The Movie is all her Uncle Fergus thinks about. He has not gone into the pharmacy for five days now and is certain that the end is soon and insists they form a united front against the establishment who plot his demise, are engineering the family's downfall. He rants that even his own flesh and blood have betrayed him.

Sheryl feels partly to blame. She has been a bad girl lately. She does not know how the badness got into her. She has been grounded for running away and stealing money, and then the other day she had words with Eleanor who stood in the hall in her satin bathrobe, saying, Do something with her, darling. So Fergus had marched her down the lane to the abattoir again, *This hurts me more than you,* where she had to spend half the night alone in the freezer to learn her lesson. And when he turned out the lights and she was plunged into a darkness so absolute there was no up or down, she heard the headless cows whispering: *We are watching you, we are watching.*

Thank goodness for daylight when hourly sunlight pales and the shadows grow longer. She knows her mind is playing tricks on her but she is not herself, Fergus will not let her sleep. It's the only way, he says, to really get into The Movie, to overcome the ego and enter the mystery fully you must leave ordinary life behind. And so he came in several times throughout the night, the light screaming on, the bloodied bodies leaping into view, the cold sucking the breath out of her, and he walked her around the yard, talking with her about the coming chaos and daring to cross over to the new world. He said he was counting on her, she was such a special girl, having the *sight* and MacRae blood and all, *remember who you are,* daughter of a long and proud lineage. He told her a story the way he often did. He said that in olden times devotees of the secret path entered the goddess Hellel's pit, and it was full of skulls and bones, snakes and spiders, and disciples spent the night there so that they might conquer their fear of death. And when they were resurrected in the morning, they had the *sight* and other exceptional gifts, they could foretell the future in dreams.

Sheryl was like that, he said, this was her training, for which she had been groomed since the age of three, and she sobbed and said that she didn't want to be special or trained or groomed, she hated spiders and skeletons and dreams. But he patted her head saying, That's my girl, and turned the light out again and she huddled in the corner with an itchy Hudson's Bay blanket around her thin arms, too frightened to speak or cry or yawn, the stink of slaughtered meat on her skin, a creepy presence in the room with her and she worried that girl from her dreams hovered somewhere close.

In the morning Earl had liberated Sheryl. She was told to get dressed quickly, was given a costume and a wig, a long fluffy blond mane that makes her look silly with her small face and buggy grey eyes, the hair huge as a country singer's. The tribe was instructed to call her Mary and the sound of this name unhinges her.

This is all part of the preparation for the Now, and she tells herself she will make it through this day if only she can keep her eyes open and not fall asleep, but nothing has been harder anytime, anywhere.

Eammon is in the cab of the truck, Sheryl can hear opera on the radio. Fergus has bought him new teeth and Eammon is obsessed with them, looks at himself constantly in every glass surface nearby. The false teeth are big and square, perfect and white as the big bellied washing machine. Truly he is more handsome and just slightly less creepy but he still stares at her constantly and covers his mouth with his hand when he talks or grins, and Sheryl thinks now it is too late, being toothless all that time has ruined him for good.

To pass the time Sheryl reads. In *The Bungalow Mystery* Laura gets rescued but Sheryl is not satisfied by the endings of her Nancy Drew mysteries anymore. She thinks the titian-haired sleuth is shallow and spoiled and ridiculously perfect. She is a rich kid with a roadster; her father lets her do whatever she wants. Her flashlight never runs out of batteries, like a cartoon she gets bludgeoned but always stands up. Sheryl feels silly now for having believed in her. Real life is much more mysterious and unfair. She closes the book and tosses it into a corner of the truck.

Up at the house, Eleanor is in the kitchen, twirling her platinum hair around a finger, a cigarette in one hand, wearing her bubble-gum coloured robe, dirty laundry in a hamper by the door, scuff marks on the floor. She hasn't been out on one of her Avon appointments for a week now and the house looks as messy and neglected as Eleanor.

Today she has a bruise on her cheek and puts a pair of sunglasses on when Sheryl comes in. In the sink, dishes are piled high as the leaning tower of Pisa Sheryl saw in a magazine once.

The radio is on and the announcer reports that Canada has adopted the single maple leaf for the new flag. More people have been taken into custody in the case of the missing civil rights workers, leading to speculation that a large group were involved.

Sheryl sits at the table and Eleanor says: I never wanted to end up out here, you know? To marry a farmer's son and move to the country. I hate all that—cows and fertilizer, dirty boots and rotting fruit. I hate apples and men with those hats with the stupid ear flaps, you know? I should never have left Pearl's Beauty Parlour. I did all the Tonis, the tinting. Behind Eleanor's sunglasses her eyes are bloodshot. Sheryl tucks her rebellious hair behind her ears and nods.

Life here is just cooking and dishes and laundry and more cooking again, you know? And MacRae craziness. She takes a drag of her cigarette and her hand trembles.

You think your Uncle Fergus knows everything, but he doesn't. He's smart, sometimes too smart for his own good, you know? I couldn't give two hoots for the horse fourmen, it's all horse manure, if you ask me. I should have left him, but where would I go?

Anywhere, I could go with you, Sheryl says. We could go together, you and me, take the car.

Eleanor chuckles, takes a drag on her cigarette. You're just a girl, Eleanor shrugs and butts out. No, she sighs, truth is, he's the only one who loves me.

The MacRae tribe is spread out on the tractor road ahead, jiggling to stay warm, Earl with the camera they call the Honeywell Elmo. Sheryl hops down from the truck and wanders over. Peter is Jesus and they are not allowed to call him anything else. Eleanor has dyed his hair butterscotch and it is long and he is bearded and beautiful just like Jesus in all the Bible pictures in Sunday school, and he looks so changed she could almost believe Peter *is* the saviour. Although Sheryl has always been suspicious of the inconsistency in the pictures of Jesus, the different faces and expressions from book to book, church to church, picture to picture, as though Jesus were really a master of disguise and everyone had seen a different guy. But she likes Peter's version, his Jesus is sexier than most of the others she's seen. Besides he is her first love and he shines above everyone everywhere anyhow.

Peter is dirty and half-naked in the autumn air, wearing a T-shirt and a flannel sheet wrapped around his waist. The others are dressed in costumes too, even Josh. They wear togas made out of old bed sheets and burlap sacks from the storage room that are supposed to make them look as though they are in the Old Testament. But the effect is ruined by weather; the sky is a watery blue, clean and pure as a swimming pool, but the air is cool and so they wear windbreakers, toques and rubber boots with their costumes. The earth is spongy and damp and smells both clean and dirty like pine cones and ditches. A crow caws. The shuffle of dead leaves accompanies their footsteps.

Fergus is excited and irritable, he strides on ahead, a megaphone at his lips, shouting directions even though they are standing only a few feet away from him. All morning he has been telling everyone who cares to listen that this is his masterpiece, this will be his best movie yet.

Jesus carries his cross along the old tractor road, stumbling every once in a while under its weight, Earl juggling the Honeywell Elmo while Peter complains that the cross is as heavy as the one the real J.C. had to carry. Fergus rolls his eyes and shouts Cut! through the megaphone.

After they do the scene a gazillion times, Peter falls with his arms wrapped around the cross like a clumsy dance partner, and this time he stays down on all fours. Fergus shouts cut again in an exasperated tone and stands rubbing his eyes, disgusted with them all. Earl puts down the camera and adjusts his toga and Sheryl wraps her fake blonde hair around her throat and wishes they would leave Peter alone. Fergus walks over to Peter crying now like a little boy, his tears forming muddy pools in the road where he has fallen. He sobs, I can't go on, blubbering that he doesn't care anymore about sex or drugs, free love or the new world, he just wants to go home. Sheryl is heartbroken that he would want to leave. But she knows about the need for a home. All at once she realizes he is only a boy blubbering for his mother, and she feels sorry for him and hates them all for being so mean.

Fergus stands in front of his Angel Boy, his tall shadow falling over the tears in the road and waits. Peter tells Fergus that he loves him, he wants to do a good job with his part in The Movie. Choking, he wipes the tears and snot from his face with the back of his skinny, grey arm. Sheryl is surprised by this outburst but knows her uncle has this effect on people, everyone wants to please him and she thinks maybe Peter hasn't slept either, feelings being so close to the skin when there is no rest in the night to sooth and cradle them in; she is also mixed up today about things.

Fergus pats Peter on the back, once, twice, gently. He smears the dirt on Jesus's forehead with long fingers, while the boy sobs, I'm too fucking tired, man, until he gets embarrassed and crying seems silly or Fergus's silence shames him and Peter says he's sorry.

Fergus hands him a tissue and says very politely, No apologies necessary, kiddo.

Josh comes over to stand by Sheryl. He is wearing a toga made out of an old potato sack and his corduroys and Hush Puppies stick out underneath. On his head he has a red toque that his orange hair rims in a little carrot-coloured fringe like Orphan Annie. He carries a staff because he is a shepherd boy, and just looking at him gives her a wrong feeling.

He whispers, What a cry baby, and she tells him to shut up. He shrugs and says, Jeez Louise, you don't have to take a hairy fit, I was only kidding, but Sheryl knows he wasn't kidding, he was being nasty, it's the collective mood today, The Movie.

I'm hungry, Josh complains, my tummy's grumbling, but she doesn't answer him, doesn't care. Oh forget it, he says wandering off.

We never talked, eh, Peter says, getting up and dusting himself off, me and my Pop. He says it like a question.

You're a good boy, Fergus says without smiling, then Fergus places the crown of thorns, which is in reality a tangled barb wire with cedar woven through, back on Peter's head while the boy wipes his face and Fergus holds the cross, waiting.

There is light, so hot, so blinding, all encompassing like God. It settles on everything around her making the girl feel safe and loved. Then she opens her eyes and blinks into pupil-drowning light. A bulb sways above. Pain crashes into her. Beyond the bulb—a dizzying blackness and a voice. Tell us your name? the voice asks. The girl frets. Sheryl? she says. There is a shock of pain. After the fourth or fifth time her name deserts her. She lies on a table, naked, suspended halfway between earth and sky, dreaming and wakefulness. Desperate, she says every name she can think of that begins with the letter A: Annie, Anabel, Annette, Anya? But none will do. They apply the shock again. Her body flexes and sizzles. A slap stains her cheek. She's not sure who she is. The bulb sways back and forth, in its centre, explosions in red and green.

It's been so long since she slept. Long past what she can bear. The shed smells of dust and mould, urine and shit. She has let go all over the table. There are wet pools under the small of her back. She cries so hard she has the hiccups.

Why are you hurting me?

Because we love you.

More questions without answers. A car passes somewhere far away. Another voice joins the first and they bend close, hissing into her ears in a malevolent duo that overlaps and sends her attention scurrying: You think you can run to Toronto and find your mommy... 11:11, the apocalypse has come ... she left you behind, she didn't want you, she doesn't love you ... you cannot go, you cannot run .... Mommy couldn't wait to get the hell out of here, she left you behind for us to bring up ... if you tell, we'll cut out your tongue ... you're nothing but white trash, the daughter of a whore ... you are already married to the dark one ...

They finish in unison: So you'll do as your told, because you're nobody, no one.

Somewhere a saw starts up with an electric whine. Clark Gable lurches into view, suspended by his rabbit ears and the girl whimpers: Please....

There's a siren shriek and blood and fur flies everywhere....

Suddenly she is falling, back through time, until a man shakes her shoulder, saying: Come here, honey. Come see the horsey.

In the barn, Eponey lies in the hay, her neck tied to the stall, her hooves pulled apart and fastened with rope. Eponey whinnies. The little girl pats the horse's wet flank saying, It's okay pony.

The man bends over the horse and thrusts. The horse screams, and the girl screams too as she's thrust inside the mare's belly, choking, gasping, blood-spattered breathless, groping in the dark tunnel of death, horse kicking death, scrabbling toward that pinprick of light: Let me out, let me out! But he doesn't let her out so finally she surrenders, slipping into that peaceful somewhere where there is no blood, no belly, no dying horse, thumb in the mouth, she drifts beyond pain....

But before the girl can slip away forever, the hand that shoved her in, hauls her back out again and she tumbles onto the bloody hay, coughing and gulping air. But it is no longer the same girl that went in. The old girl is trapped and floating in the horse's belly, a belly which heaves up and down now slowly, more slowly still...

This new girl can hardly see for the blood in her eyes. She blinks repeatedly, catatonic, shaking. The second man takes a knife and slices open the mare's neck. The skin parts smoothly like sliced liver, life escaping through the open seam, blood puddling in a dark pool in the hay. In one deft stroke, Eponey's terror-struck eyes go flat, black, still as a doll's eyes, lifeless as plastic.

Eponey.

Holding a bucket under the mare's head, the man catches the blood. He places his hand in the bucket and marks the girl with it—a child somewhere in the barn, crying—marking her head, her mouth, her pee-pee place and heart. As he does so he tells her that the girl she was has died, she has been reborn. He says that this is the old way. She is very special. As he smears the blood on her body he gives her a new name.

What is your name? the voice asks.

What is my name? the girl shrieks.

And the man says: You have no will of your own. Your life is ours. You do what you're told. Your name is Mary Magdalene.

Sheryl awakens somewhere halfway across the yard, the sky a grey malevolent face. It's hard to stand up straight, and in the washroom there was blood. She wants to wash but someone somewhere has told her to go feed the dog, and she can hear Lupus going crazy, barking himself hoarse again at a tractor trailer passing on the road, as though his barking could pay them all back for the one fruit truck that didn't slow down and mashed his puppy legs, making him a cripple for life.

She can see the spittle along his jaw, his canine eyes, baby blue, glassy and transparent as marbles, and his raspy bark is raw and grating, but she doesn't yell at him. He isn't barking at her, she's figured that much out. While he paces the length of his chain, she totters into the barn not sure if she slept last night or where or how long, she is afraid to look at anything too closely. She shuffles like a robot, *keep moving,* and grabs Lupus's slop pail. Sound hurts. As the kibble clamours into the bowl she holds her ears. Leaves the colour of fire engines scuttle and whisper. She wants to shriek. Only the trees in the orchard are quiet, their arms cold and black, leafless and stunned by autumn. She trundles back outside and realizes only then that she has that silly red velvet robe on over her pants and rubber boots and she thinks, today I'm Mary Magdalene and remembers, The Movie, and suddenly she is not so sure who she is anymore or what's going on.

The truck has gone and Lupus is by his doghouse waiting for her, but she doesn't look at him, doesn't think. She stumbles through the yard and into his territory, placing the food bowl not far from him, too tired to be afraid, and miraculously he doesn't growl or attack, just sits and waits. Licks his bum. She plunks herself down in the dirt too, collapsing and puts her head on her knees and cries her heart out. She doesn't know why she's crying but her sadness has something to do with her mother and the horse's head door knocker. Her world is spinning into chaos, and she feels lost and is sure somehow it is her fault. She hears a noise and peeks through her arms and sees Lupus, his pink tongue lolling, his wild wolf eyes staring through her to the wild beyond, crouching not a foot from her, panting. She hopes he bites her head off, and she dies right here, right now. She could sleep then. But he doesn't. As if he knows, senses something. She cries some more and when she's finished she talks to him, without looking in his eyes so that she doesn't get sucked into the wide open spaces there. He shimmies his broken bum forward as if to hear her better and tenderly licks her fingers: once, twice. Then he groans and lies down. And all at once she knows: Lupus isn't the crazy one.

Sheryl runs into Josh in the yard and he is morose, he doesn't want to be a boring shepherd boy.

Why has everybody gone mental all of a sudden? he complains and Sheryl snaps, You should talk. Cat skinner. He hangs his head and they walk on down the old tractor road in silence.

Now that harvest is over I guess Pete will move on, Josh says. But Sheryl doesn't know.

They find the others huddled by the barbecue pit, hanging out like in summer, in the good old days of the hootenannies, Earl fiddling with the new Honeywell Elmo pocket zoom 83 movie camera while Eammon and Eleanor sit on the logs at the pit flirting shamelessly, drinking Earl's dandelion wine and singing campfire songs.

If I had a hammer
I'd hammer in the morning
I'd hammer in the evening
All over this land …

They nod at Sheryl and Josh briefly as the children set themselves before the small fire. April isn't with them. According to Earl, she had a bad case of nerves a while back and they had to take her to hospital. The doctors don't know yet when she can come home.

Eleanor giggles as she and Eammon blow each other a kiss. Sheryl can see the others out by Kitchenhenge. Fergus is all dressed up in his new director clothes which consist of black slacks and turtleneck, a red and purple cape and a huge cross and pentacle around his neck in honour of the two gods. Earl joins them and Fergus yells: Action! Earl zooms in on Peter playing a thin, stoned saviour prone to fits of giggling. Josh reluctantly plays the shepherd boy again, and Sheryl is asked to put on the long blonde wig with its Bo-Peep curls. She kneels on the frost-hardened ground before the unsteady Jesus and says: We've chosen you to be the King of the Jews, our God-King, and the others, now a ragtaggle of extras in their impossible costumes of sweaters and togas with running shoes poking beneath, like biblical hippies, come rushing forward waving plastic palm fronds at the grinning, foolish teenager until Fergus yells, Cut! and they fall over each other killing themselves laughing.

The bulb sways and in it's centre a voice: Who are you?
*   I am nobody, the girl says. I do what I'm told.*
*   The headless cows in the freezer are her friends. In the darkness she can almost hear them lowing.*

In the black-and-white room of Sheryl's mind, the lights are off and she is watching The Movie. The movie of The Movie. The lights from the projector flash off and on. Ticka ticka ticka. She sees the pink-and-white-checked tablecloth flutter over the picnic table. Sheryl helps Eleanor hand out brightly-coloured plastic plates, cutlery and cloth napkins. Her fingers are busy robots, her body walks about mechanically. The others dig in. Eammon takes his new teeth out to chew, and the teeth sit on the corner of the tablecloth looking as though they might speak.
    Ticka ticka ticka.
    Jesus is allowed none of the regular food. A hand slaps away his drumstick. Suddenly Fergus appears. He offers a beautiful ripe McIntosh. Dish of the immortals. The apple twists and turns in his palm. Fergus's face leers on screen, and he begins his speech.
    The ancients believed that in the course of a year there wasn't just one, but two suns in the sky. They thought the waxing sun, which grew warmer from winter solstice to summer solstice, was a different sun from the thin, cool and distant waning one that reigned the wintry months of the year. Primitive peoples believed the sun's seasonal changes happened because the waxing sun was destroyed by a bloody insurrection every year. They worshipped the sun as a king. According to them, the sun king, or waxing sun, was ritually slain by his successor, the waning sun, who was then ritually slaughtered in turn, *ad infinitum*, in an endless war of succession in the heavens, with each passing solstice.
    Fergus's face shrinks and grows, going in and out of focus.

Think of it, Fergus's voice continues, the camera zooming in on the apple swivelling in his palm. They re-enacted this event in the sky by picking a sun king to rule on earth for half a year. When the sun king was at the end of his reign, he went to a sacred grove after the harvest, and there he was given a ritual meal of apples, the last meal of a condemned man. But you see, the apples were a solace to him, because *malus domestica*—the apple—is the tree of life and the sun king knew that by eating the fruit he was blessed and would gain immortality and so he accepted his fate. After the meal he was tortured and his blood was spilt. The ritual murder ensured the growth of crops the following year, it cleansed the whole community, provided an Aristotelian catharsis that enervated the entire village.

The Honeywell Elmo ticks on, ticka ticka ticka. A mischievous wind sends the napkins scurrying.

Fergus carries on: This is the first story, the story of Bacchus Liber, the wine god, of Osiris the Egyptian, and his reborn son Horus, of the man we know as Christus the Jew, gods all who were tortured and dismembered, their blood spilt for the general good and who rose again, resurrected and immortal. Earl zooms in on the pharmacist, who takes a bow in his wild grape-coloured cape with the shiny red lining.

Time crawls by. The picnic table is cold for sitting, the green paint chipped. Sheryl clutches a spoon and wishes she could sleep while sitting, eyes open. She wants to sleep so badly there is no room for any other thoughts. She walks and talks, but her own body is a stranger to her. She closes her eyes, and her curly Bo-Peep head nods until Josh sings into her ear: *They're coming to take you away, ha!ha!* and she startles and falls off the bench.

Suddenly Earl is there with a squawking chicken, feet tied, hanging upside down. Earl walks over to a log in the woodpile. The chicken clucks quietly, mesmerized by its upside-down world. Earl swings the bird into the air and thwacks the body onto the stump. Feathers fly. The axe comes down and makes two halves of its neck. The head topples into the grass, still squawking. Earl holds the twitching body, as the hot liquid of the fowl's life flowers red into a bowl.

There's your wine, Earl says plonking the bowl onto the table.

Sheryl throws up all over a small shrub. When she's finished, she wipes her mouth on her jacket sleeve, and someone offers her a drink. There is crying and swearing and then silence.

There's something she's not remembering, it's as if someone lurks over her shoulder and whispers into her ear, but when she turns around she sees nothing. As if she has left the house without something she needs. It is hard to focus, hard to see. She stares at the tablecloth trying to remember.

The room goes black. Ticka ticka ticka. The clapper board reads: Take 12, The Last Supper.

Jesus says: This is the last meal I'm going to sit down and share with all of you, and the disciples protest, banging their fists. Jesus, crown of thorns slipping, takes a piece of Wonderbread.

This bread is my body, he says, when you eat this bread, you're eating me.

Giggling. He dips the bread into the steaming chicken's blood, his face wrinkling.

Ticka, ticka.

Jesus says: This is my blood, when you drink this wine you drink of me.

He takes a gulp and spits it into the grass.

The camera follows Eleanor and Jesus walking in an open field. Eleanor wears sunglasses, pigtails and a long flowing dress that makes her look like Maid Marian. She smiles a hard painted smile. She hands Peter a piece of rubber, a spoon and a syringe. Jesus gives a little whoop and wraps the rubber around his arm, holds a lighter under a spoon, slides the needle in.

Okay, Earl says interrupting them, now we nail you to the cross.

Peter protests, his words slurring, his eyes half-lidded. The camera spins and discovers tears on Eleanor's cheeks.

Come on, man, Peter complains off-camera, can't we call it a day?

Earl pushes the boy towards the cross, snorting: Get a move on Nazarene.

Sheryl and Pete,
Sitting in a tree,
KISSING.
First comes love,
Then comes marriage,
Here comes Sheryl in a baby carriage!

She-eryl! Sheryl's mother stands on the front porch of the past, calling her in for dinner. Sheryl plays hide-and-go-seek with her imaginary friend in an open field. The grass grows over her head, it sings and makes her legs itch when she runs. It smells like summer, dry and warm, like wildflowers and earthworms and skipping ropes. Co-oming! she yells back at her mommy, but the little girl is still hiding and doesn't come.

On a dirt floor in a shed, the girl watches a small beast, muzzled, harnessed and trapped. White candles flicker. Shadows of yard tools leapfrog along the walls.

Beast! Beast! the voices chant. Every which way the beast turns it is attacked, poked, slapped and yelled at. Wearing a black leather vest, bum bare, tied to the table with a lead and dog collar, the beast dives under the table legs for cover, but is repeatedly hauled out and tormented.

The girl watches from above, sitting safe and high on a shelf. She shakes her head at the beast, poor doggy dog, she's glad it isn't her, but she won't come down, can't help.

Outside, the sky rains fire and there is the clip-clop of hooves, the four horsemen coming....

A circle of light. At its centre, a body. All around the body, a halo of visible heat, a yellow rim of pain, where life leaks into death. Beyond, the air is chill and so black. Looking at the body brings the girl grief. The boy is mounted on a cross. Lit brilliantly by stage lights.

Fergus! Jesus wails, and someone swaggers out of the impenetrable darkness and steps into the ring of light, half-naked but for rubber boots and a flannel sheet tied around his waist. On his forehead is painted the all-seeing eye and he wears black-rimmed glasses and the antlers of the Faery King. There are slashes of blue paint across his cheeks. He is electric with excitement and paces, unable to stand still, skipping on long, thin, hairy legs.

The Saviour begs in a whisper, teeth chattering in pain: Get me down from here, man. His hands are pulpy, fat and swollen, blood drips along his fingers, down the cross, forming damp dark pools in the grass. He is sweating and shivering in his yellow halo.

Black water, the girl says, I told you so, but Sheryl puts her hands over her eyes. I can't see you, she says, I'm nobody, I'm not here, I'm not listening.

You should thank me, the satyr yells, in the moon glare of the light. Before you met me you were just another loser, a runaway, a hitchhiker. By dying on the cross, I confer upon you the status of Osiris, the Egyptian God who died and was reborn. You are blessed. You have been chosen.

The boy groans.

Think of the eternal, the dark one says, shaking his long, delicate hands in the night air, his painted face shimmering. You're starring in the greatest movie of all, kiddo. The story that has riveted the world for centuries.

The blood drips, the girl can't stop staring at the black water.

Oh God, the boy cries.

The mad sprite cackles, jigging in the trampled grass, the camera zooming in on his face, ticka, ticka.

Your Jesus Christ is nothing but a fiction created from myths and legends of all the other heathens of the old world. Even his miracles were stolen from the deities who came before him: healing the sick, raising the dead, casting out devils, all commonplace miracles performed by roving charlatans exactly like the gurus and yogis and faith-healers of the new age we find ourselves in now.

When your King of Kings lived, every beggar and vagabond in Jerusalem called himself the son of god. Your Shepherd of Shepherds was none other than the god/king the Jews selected every spring for sacrifice in order to ensure a good crop. The Honeywell Elmo goes ticka, ticka, ticka.

The Saviour pleads, Please, I'll do whatever ....

I want my Jesus to die on the cross, the dark one says.

Drip, drip, ticka, ticka.

The saviour sobs.

Ah, Jesus-boy, the Faery King continues fondly, You've come to a sad state. Seems to me you've broken a few golden rules. Tsk, tsk, the flesh is weak. Why should I show you mercy? Together we're righting the wrongs of two thousand years of history.

Beast! Beast! the voices shriek, swooping and thrusting on nimble feet, maddening their prey, calling the king of darkness into the beast, poking and teasing and enraging.

Poor doggy dog, the girl says.

Sheryl cups her eyes with her hands: I'm not looking, I'm not listening.

The beast obeys with hissing and spitting. The night explodes with sound and people. The small carnival of stoned gypsies out in the field begins a procession around the circle of light: banging drums, dancing and whooping. Chanting: Here comes the beast!

The boy is lowered from the cross. He rolls onto his back cradling bloody hands, curling broken feet. Candles twinkle like fireflies. The girl watches from afar as the revellers join the lighted circle, dragging a mad dog on a leash. They blow on flutes, spank drums, but for a moment it is silent in the girl's black-and-white world.

There is a flurry of activity: hair and leather, arms and hips and skin and teeth. The beast is prodded toward the saviour. Their bodies wrestle in the slap of movie lights. A lock of hair escapes from the beast's leather helmet, a thin, twisted

Then she is running. Sheryl-Anne MacRae runs along the old tractor road, thundering along the path on dirty sneakered feet, running, panting, the only sound her own breath, which thumps along with her heart, a wild beat so loud she's sure the whole forest can hear it: *Only so many beats to a life, 1 2 3 4 5 6 ... Fergus says: I had a dream of a goat and a lamb, I am the Beast, I am HE; MEOW goes the kitty in the trunk of the car, does anybody hear anything?* Sunday night is always Ed Sullivan. *Tonight we're going to have a really big show ... kees me Eddie, kees me good night.*

The world is still and chilly and silent, languishing between fall and spring, the orchard dark and barren in the distance. She thumps along the frosty terrain of the open field without looking back, feet cold and sockless in red sneakers, stumbling, the night's indifferent bowl of stars wheeling overhead. It is quiet and safe, but Sheryl is alone under the enormous space of the night's mysterious dome. She plunges into the orchard, rushing through the tidy rows of Northern Spys, hidden within the dark chiselled arms of the furthermost Niagara block, embraced by the dark damp smell of rotting leaves and soil.

Hurry, hurry, run, run.

She throws the barn door open, something must be saved: for one death, a life.

Hot tears fall onto her hands, she gets the cage doors open and one by one lifts out the rabbits: Vivian, the smoky Netherland dwarf, the New Zealand whites, Grace and Kelly, with their pink-veined ears and albino eyes. They are fat and drowsy and annoyed by her interruption of their nightly sleep. She sets them loose on the barn floor and shoos them out the door with a broom.

Lupus is berserk with barking, murderous and thrilled by the sight of the rabbits, their long, gentle ears and fat, furry bodies hopping in the moonlight out in the yard.

She slinks along his dirt circle, grabs the end of his chain. It takes a minute, but miraculously he is free and bolting like a white rocket, bursting in a frenzy of joyous barking, scattering the rabbits across the lawn.

Sheryl locks all the doors, showers and grabs the old pink valise and tiptoes down the stairs. She grabs a flashlight in the hall, she is her own sleuth now. She stashes the suitcase in the front closet and creeps down the basement stairs. She stops outside Fergus's photography studio, and stands panting outside the door, so frightened she can feel every hair on her head, her fear so huge, it has nails and teeth. She jiggles the door knob but the door is locked. She gets up on a chair and runs her hands above the door frame and the key is there. Thank you, Nancy Drew. She unlocks the door and it swings wide. Her knees buckle. The walls are painted black and on them is scrawled a purple-and-red riot of sayings, symbols, numbers and pictures: a swastika and a cross, an eye in a triangle, the words: Blue Power, DRUID, Kali-Yuga, *Novus Ordo Sec* and beside the Latin, New World Order. Numbers everywhere: 666, 1, 3, 5, 7, and 11:11.

On the wall opposite is a picture of a decapitated goat's head, bleeding, so real it seems alive, and a cross with Jesus on it. Below them is written: I AM GOD, Two Gods, FUCK THE ESTABLISHMENT and The Time is Now.

A skull, perches on a desk, facing the door, tiny and bleached with the word MOLLOCH written on it.

A wind rattles the house then a Sunday morning quiet descends. Sheryl's breathing calms. Beyond this room is another bathed in darkness, the door ajar, a smell rank and chlorinated like a swimming pool. She walks towards the door, opens it, the hinges complain a little. Inside is her Uncle Fergus's darkroom, his laboratory, the birthplace of his masterpieces, his genius, and she frets for a moment in the doorway. A bulb hangs from the ceiling. She pulls the string and the dark room is illuminated.

There are three tubs of fluid, they shine blue and chemical green in the pale light, beside them a shelf piled high with lenses, filters and film. Above the two tubs there is a clothesline with photographs, large black-and-whites blown up and hanging from clothes pins to dry. She looks at one and sees Peter, a raft of photographs of the boy, all stark-naked. She gasps going from one to the other: Peter with an erection, Peter with Eleanor, Peter with Fergus, all of them together in different sexual poses, with cartoon smiles, wearing nothing but hats and sneakers.

Sheryl is shaking as she moves to the tubs.

Floating in the first tub like some freakish apparition: herself, naked, lying on a slab of marble, asleep, black hair in a disordered corona. Her hands are tied. A white dress on the floor beside her. She stares at herself shimmering and waving in fluid. The others are dressed in robes, holding candles. It is her family, the whole MacRae tribe. She looks up. The walls are papered with photos, in little frames, some of her, some of other children, and they are all there: all the hitchhikers and hobos and lost souls that Fergus has picked up over the years, the familiar faces peering wide-eyed from the shocking past, even Ralph MacDonald, bruised and grimacing. Fergus used them all. And then one in particular catches her eye—a very old photo, yellowed and curling on the edges. In it, a filthy, bloodied child crouches beside the head of a horse. Two men with her. Her Uncle Fergus and Grandpa MacRae. The child stares out at Sheryl with huge, woeful eyes, black and blind.

She is out the door in minutes and on Josh's cycle, the blue CCM, the valise dangling from the carrier, riding down the drive through the dawn, all along the still and empty tenth line, through the county roads, cycling fast, chasing the creeping light, above her the great troubled map of the sky. When she enters Cedar Hollow, Sheryl sails along the small town streets wearing their early morning silence like indifference.

She will go somewhere far away, tell someone, anyone. Although who will believe her?

Sheryl weaves the CCM in and out of the white lines of the meridian. They climb the hill in short white jabs, arrows expanding like the dawn, pointing the way toward a new and better world.

Acknowledgements

This book is the result of the faith and support of many people over many years. For the initial Canadian Doubleday edition, I want to thank The Canada Council and the Ontario Arts Council for grants that gave me the necessary writing time. I also want to rethank: the late Timothy Findley, Janis Rapoport, Denise Bukowski, Martha Kanye-Forstner and all the wonderful people at Doubleday; as well as those helpful good-natured apple farmers in Simcoe and Grey-Bruce County, who shared their love of Eve's fruit and were not at all like the people in my book. A shout out to Maya Mavjee for giving me my first break, and Sally Cooper and John Albanis for working so hard to make *Mad Dog* into a movie. For this second U.S. edition, I want to say gracias to Lynda Schor, who introduced me to HSE and kept encouraging me to reprint this book. Thanks to Carole Rosenthal for saying yes, to Tasha Paley for reminding me that writing can be service, and to Meredith Sue Willis for her endless technical and publishing help. Thanks also to my newfound tribe, the WWRITERS, (women writers in transit), for the talks and tea and support. Finally, many thanks to Allan, as always, for pushing me to go ahead and always being in my corner.

Mad Dog Reading Guide:
Questions and Topics for Discussion

1. The main character of Mad Dog is the precocious fourteen-year-old protagonist Sheryl-Anne MacRae. In what ways does she seem childlike and in others older than her years? Why is she living on her uncle's farm? What does she long for? How does this longing motivate her actions?

2. The story opens with the arrival of a stranger--the guitar-toting Peter Lucas Angelo. Why does she take such a shine to Peter? How does her Uncle encourage that relationship and/or interfere with it? How does Sheryl's relationship with Peter change throughout the book? What role does Eleanor play in that?

3. Sheryl's Uncle Fergus tells her that she has the sight and throughout the book Sheryl has visions. Describe them. How do they change as the story develops? Who is the *girl* and what is she trying to tell Sheryl?

4.The book takes place in the year 1964—the summer of race riots, mini-skirts and transistor radios. What do you know about this time period? A pivotal news event occurs as backdrop to that summer—what is it? Is racism alive and well in Cedar Hollow? How is it related to the language? Are there any parallels to what's happening in North America today?

5.The location of the book is rural apple country in Ontario. What's the significance of the apple in the story? How does the remote location affect what takes place on the farm? Could these events have taken place in any other place or time?

6. Discuss the meaning of the title: *Mad Dog*. Who is the mad dog in the book? Why is Lupus mad? How does he change throughout the novel? What is Sheryl's relationship to Lupus? Who is the mad dog in the end? How does Lupus tie into Sheryl's liberation?

7. Sheryl's Uncle Fergus is a powerful character in the book. He is described as a photographer, pharmacist and good Samaritan. What do we learn about him over the course of the summer? Is he evil? Is he

truly religious? What is his main philosophy? What role do his end-of-the-world beliefs play in his actions? What are the magical re-enactments in the book? Who is the real good Samaritan?

8. The style of the book was described by one reviewer as Southern Ontario Gothic. What resonates about that description? Does the style serve the story?

9. The first edition of the book was launched by Doubleday, September 2001, right after 9-11, so the book was published only in Canada and largely ignored. Do the issues of sexual predation, child pornography and racism in the book still resonate? How has public perception of child sexual abuse changed over the last two decades? What is different about this book from others you've read on a similar subject? What did you learn about predators and their techniques?

10. Did you find the novel painful to read? How would Sheryl's fate have been different if this had happened today? Was the book educational or informative in any way?

About the Author

Kelly Watt's award-winning short stories have been anthologized, published internationally and longlisted for the prestigious CBC Radio's Short Fiction Contest twice (2017/2015). She is the author of two books—the travel companion *Camino Meditations* (2014), and the gothic novel *Mad Dog (2019)*. Originally published in 2001, *Mad Dog* was a Globe and Mail notable book. This is the revised U.S. edition. Watt lives in the Ontario countryside with her husband, a miniature schnauzer and three diligent chickens.